Michael Underwood and The Murder Room

>>> This title is part of The Murder Room, our series dedicated to making available out-of-print or hard-to-find titles by classic crime writers.

Crime fiction has always held up a mirror to society. The Victorians were fascinated by sensational murder and the emerging science of detection; now we are obsessed with the forensic detail of violent death. And no other genre has so captivated and enthralled readers.

Vast troves of classic crime writing have for a long time been unavailable to all but the most dedicated frequenters of second-hand bookshops. The advent of digital publishing means that we are now able to bring you the backlists of a huge range of titles by classic and contemporary crime writers, some of which have been out of print for decades.

From the genteel amateur private eyes of the Golden Age and the femmes fatales of pulp fiction, to the morally ambiguous hard-boiled detectives of mid twentieth-century America and their descendants who walk our twenty-first century streets, The Murder Room has it all. **>>>**

The Murder Room
Where Criminal Minds Meet

themurderroom.com

Michael Underwood (1916–1992)

Michael Underwood (the pseudonym of John Michael Evelyn) was born in Worthing, Sussex and educated at Christ Church College, Oxford. He was called to the Bar in 1939 and served in the British army during World War Two. He returned to work in the Department of Public Prosecutions until his retirement in 1976, and wrote almost 50 crime novels informed by his career in the law. His five series characters include Sergeant Nick Atwell and lawyer Rosa Epton, of whom is was said by the *Washington Post* that she 'outdoes Perry Mason'.

By Michael Underwood

The Unprofessional Spy

Michael Underwood

An Orion book

Copyright © Isobel Mackenzie 1964

The right of Michael Underwood to be identified as the author of this
work has been asserted in accordance with the Copyright, Designs and
Patents Act 1988.

This edition published by
The Orion Publishing Group Ltd
Orion House
5 Upper St Martin's Lane
London WC2H 9EA

An Hachette UK company
A CIP catalogue record for this book is available from the British Library

ISBN 978 1 4719 0796 8

www.orionbooks.co.uk

For Hugh and Alex Clough

MR. JUSTICE PENREY's firmly masculine hands caressed the arms of his deep leather chair. With head rested against its high back, his expression was contemplative as his glance fell idly around him. He might have been relaxing in the smoking-room of his club after dinner, and it required only a small flight of imagination actually to smell his cigar. In fact he was in Number 1 Court at the Old Bailey, and about to sentence a man to twenty years' imprisonment.

He acknowledged the end of defending counsel's plea in mitigation with the merest inclination of his head and brought his gaze round to the man in the dock, who was now standing up and facing him impassively across the short divide which separated judge from judged.

Impassivity had marked the prisoner's conduct throughout the trial. He was a man of about forty-five, with a square face and a figure which could best be described as sturdy. Thick, black hair was brushed straight back from an even line and accentuated the squareness of his features. His eyes now met the judge's without flinching. There was neither fear nor servility in his expression. His counsel might plead for mercy but the prisoner himself appeared detached and with patient resignation to be waiting only for the inescapable finale.

Resting his fingertips on the edge of the desk in front of him, Mr. Justice Penrey leaned slightly forward and began speaking, selecting his words as if they were precious stones from a chest of treasure:

'Frederick George Crofton, the jury have rightly convicted you of espionage, for it must be abundantly clear to anyone who has listened to the evidence in this case that you are a spy. A professional spy, moreover, of unquestioned skill and tenacity whose operations in this country have made you a menace to each of its citizens. Little, it seems, is known about you: who you are, how you came to these shores, and it may well be that your true identity will remain for all time hidden in the mists which inevitably shroud the activities of those engaged in espionage. You have been ably defended by Mr. Ainsworth in accordance with the best traditions of our Bar, and he has said everything which could possibly be advanced on your behalf, but the result could never have been in any doubt. It is now my duty to impose a sentence which will not only bring to an end your own career as a spy, but which may also serve to deter others from accepting the perils of your avocation. You will go to prison for ten years on each of the two counts. The sentences will be consecutive, making twenty years in all.'

Almost before the judge's last words had died away, the prisoner had given him a small, stiff bow—the bow of an opponent acknowledging no more than a transient personal defeat—and turning briskly on his heel had vanished down the steps at the back of the dock, leaving his escort, so it seemed, to follow or not as he chose.

Martin Ainsworth slowly gathered up his papers, though he knew that Edward, the chambers' junior clerk, would appear at any moment and see that nothing was left behind. The courtroom had emptied quickly—the bigger the case the quicker it emptied, he had had occasion to notice before—and now only a few small knots of people remained within its claustrophobic confines. Mr. Gifford, his instructing solicitor, thrust a final bundle of documents into his brief-case and turned to Ainsworth.

'Can't say I was surprised by the sentence,' he remarked in a tone which seemed to indicate that he, for one, regarded himself as a law-abiding citizen recently menaced by his client's activities. 'Don't see that the judge could have given him any less.'

Martin Ainsworth smiled noncommittally. Though there was nothing to argue about, he couldn't have brought himself then to express agreement. Twenty years' imprisonment was the rational reply to Crofton's conduct, he knew that as well as anyone, but for the moment he was filled only with compassion for a man about whom he admittedly knew previous little but who had impressed him enormously by his courage and dignity.

'I think I ought to go and see him,' he said quietly.

'Well, if you really think we should,' Mr. Gifford observed doubtfully.

'I wasn't meaning to speak for both of us. But when a client has just received twenty years, I feel the least his counsel can do is go and show his face. If he says anything which requires your professional attention, I can let you know.'

Mr. Gifford looked relieved. 'If that's all right then, I won't accompany you. I have an appointment back in the office and I'd like to get away.'

'Of course.'

'I hope he has the good manners to thank you for your efforts on his behalf.'

'I think he probably will, though I'm darned certain I shouldn't if I were in his place.'

Mr. Gifford brushed the reservation aside as an unworthy flippancy. 'I, at any rate, should like to thank you, Mr. Ainsworth. I've much appreciated our association on this difficult and distasteful case.' He picked up his brief-case from the table. 'I'm sure we've both done our best, but I've disliked every minute of it and I'm glad it's all over. I know one is trained as a lawyer to take the detached and objective view, particularly in criminal defence work, but I'd sooner defend the most depraved murderer or rapist than I would another spy.'

'I'm certain our client never divined your feelings anyway,' Ainsworth replied stoutly. 'Incidentally, what about a possible appeal?'

'Surely not!' the solicitor exclaimed in a horrified tone. 'On what conceivable grounds?'

'I agree, I doubt whether there are any, but he may want to. After all, with twenty years inside ahead of him, he's nothing to lose.'

'I suppose he may want to appeal against sentence,' Mr. Gifford conceded. 'But he can't possibly against conviction.' In sudden embarrassment he added, 'I'm so sorry, I shouldn't have spoken like that. I shall obviously be guided by your advice when you've had an opportunity of considering the position.'

'And when we know Crofton's own feelings. . . .'

The court-room was empty by the time Martin Ainsworth let himself into the dock and nimbly descended the stairs which led to the cells below.

'Hello, Mr. Ainsworth,' the chief prison officer greeted him with a cheerful smile. 'Want to see your chap, do you?'

'How's he taken it?'

'Without a murmur. Must say you've got to hand it to him,

3

though I suppose he's been trained in a pretty tough school. Anyway, a fair trial and twenty years is a good deal better treatment than he'd have got in a great many countries, including, I have no doubt, his own.'

Crofton was sitting upright on his cell bench, with his hands resting in his lap, gazing steadily at the wall in front of him. He wore the same air of trained alertness that seemed as much a part of him as the pores of his skin. It was superimposed over every other mood and must have been the product of unceasing mental concentration.

'Ah, Mr. Ainsworth,' he said in his accentless English, as the barrister entered. 'Let me shake you by the hand to show that I bear you no grudge.'

'I'm glad of that,' Ainsworth remarked dryly. 'I did warn you that it would be a severe sentence if you were convicted.'

'You did. You also told me to expect conviction, so you were doubly right. Nevertheless'—his expression was suddenly painfully sad—'twenty years. . . . It's a very long time when you're over fifty. Inevitably one wonders . . .' It was the nearest approach to emotion Ainsworth had seen him display and it lasted no more than seconds. What followed was even more surprising. 'We gave Greville Wynne only eight years,' he said with a wry smile.

It was the first time in all their meetings that Crofton had given so much as a passing hint of the country of his origin. Up to this moment his front had been that of the English business man engaged in running a small import–export agency from an office in Holborn. And this front he had stoically maintained despite the erosive evidence of one witness after another which had been to show that he was a high-grade spy particularly concerned with Britain's NATO secrets.

'But Greville Wynne wasn't allowed the privilege of pleading not guilty,' Ainsworth said in a mildly chiding tone, his lawyer's quickness of mind overcoming his surprise.

Crofton made a small gesture of impatience. 'The British are obsessed by the appearance of fair play. I think I would sooner plead guilty and serve eight years than be convicted— you will remember, Mr. Ainsworth, that the judge said the result of the case had always been inevitable—and serve twenty. Wouldn't you?' His mood became lighter again. 'But I like the British. I have lived in London a number of years now and think of it—I hope this doesn't affront you, Mr. Ainsworth—as my other home. I've been happy here and can at least reflect that I have rewarded the people of this country for their many kindnesses to me by providing them with a splendid court case to read about. I couldn't do more than that for them, though I confess I would prefer not to have done so.'

He finished speaking and his steady gaze remained on Ainsworth's face.

'Do you wish to appeal if that is possible?' Martin Ainsworth asked, feeling that a change of subject would be tactful.

'Do I have to say now?'

'No, we have fourteen days in which to lodge notice of appeal, and one can usually get an extension of time after that.'

'I thought you had to have grounds for appeal,' Crofton said sardonically.

'You do.'

'What are mine?'

'I can't say until I've studied the transcript of the judge's summing-up.'

'But nothing has occurred to you?'

'Frankly, no.'

'Then why appeal?'

'You could always lodge a notice of appeal against sentence, and meanwhile I'll be consulting with Mr. Gifford on the possibility of appealing against conviction, too.'

'I would like to think about it.' In a reflective tone, he added, 'But I suppose I shall have to appeal.'

Martin Ainsworth thought it likely that the code-book for Soviet spies covered every contingency, including the limits to be attempted when enmeshed in another country's legal machinery. It was presumably remembrance of this which had prompted Crofton's sudden afterthought.

Ainsworth held out his hand. 'Goodbye—and good luck.'

'Thank you, Mr. Ainsworth. I hope I wasn't too embarrassing a client.'

Martin Ainsworth decided to walk back to chambers. When time permitted he enjoyed walking in London, and for short distances it was probably the quickest means of getting from one point to another. What with walking, and tennis at the weekends (he was an old Oxford blue), he managed to keep pretty fit and was still able to sprint for a bus without feeling he had brought death ten years closer, which was more than most of his contemporaries could claim to do.

In fact there was no need for him to return to chambers at all: it was the last week of the summer term and his table was virtually clear. But habit died hard, and unless there were special reasons for not doing so, he always did put in an evening appearance after court even though he knew that nothing awaited his attention. Perhaps the most cogent reason was that John, the chief clerk of chambers, expected it, and Martin Ainsworth had grown up in the law under John's pervasive influence.

It was a close, overcast evening, and the air seemed to reek more strongly than ever of exhaust fumes from the homegoing traffic. It was like breathing vaporised soup. He decided to take a slightly longer route and walk along the Embankment. There at least the smell of burnt diesel oil mingled with more astringent odours from the river.

He was beginning to feel the physical reaction which invariably set in after a heavily fought case. It was the equivalent of five sets of singles. You didn't notice it so much at the time, but once it was over every muscle wanted to remind one of its existence. And the Crofton case had been particularly exhausting.

In the first place he had done it alone without a leader—not that he had wanted one, and had indeed told Mr. Gifford he would sooner undertake the defence on his own, even though he had known that the Attorney-General would be leading for the Crown, assisted by two of the Old Bailey Treasury Counsel. To the lay eye this might have appeared to be overweighting the case against Crofton, but Ainsworth knew that in fact it would act to his advantage. One of the problems for the defence in spy trials is to induce the spy-catchers, or those of them who are reluctantly pushed forward out of the shadows, to give one any information on the side, but with the Chief Law Officer of the Crown taking personal responsibility for the conduct of the prosecution, pettifogging security-mindedness was swept from Ainsworth's path. Moreover, it was further to Crofton's advantage that he was defended by an experienced and extremely well-liked member of the Bar.

On the other hand, as he now paused and gazed at a string of coal barges being tugged up river, he couldn't avoid the sardonic reflection that Crofton could scarcely be worse off if he had been defended by the brashest nincompoop the Temple had ever produċed. He turned and stared at the distant dome of the Old Bailey topped by its golden figure of justice. She looked immaculate. Somewhere beneath her feet sat a man impassively waiting to be taken away to begin a twenty-year sentence.

It was true that the evidence against him had been overwhelming and that no other result had been possible, so what use had his defending counsel been? Ainsworth pondered this as he continued his walk beside the river. The only answer which came to his mind was that by his knowledge and experience, justice had been able to put up a better show than is sometimes the case. But was this anything more than an admission of the validity of Crofton's taunt about the British being obsessed with the appearance of fair play? Ainsworth wondered. Anyway, whatever his feelings about Crofton the man, he disapproved of his spying activities as heartily as Mr. Gifford and the judge and all the other vicariously menaced citizens.

Apart from John, sitting eternally vigilant in the clerk's office, chambers appeared deserted, though Ainsworth knew this was a false impression and that behind most of the closed doors conferences were under way which would probably be reflected later in trials leading in their turn to damages, decrees nisi, injunctions, writs, fines and even imprisonment. This was the hour of the day when the Temple's air throbbed with the hatching of plans of campaign.

'I'm sorry I couldn't get along to court, sir, to hear the end,' John said as Martin Ainsworth appeared in the doorway.

'You missed nothing. Old Penrey had been waiting three days to dot him twenty years.'

'I'm told he handled the trial very fairly.'

'Impeccably. With evidence as strong as that against the prisoner, he didn't even have to resort to innuendo, or any of those renowned facial gestures, none of which ever get on to a transcript.'

'You sound bitter, sir.'

Ainsworth smiled. 'I'm not really, though it would probably be the most becoming mood after a client has been given twenty years.'

'He'd have been shot without trial in his own country most likely.'

'That certainly seems to be the popular view,' Ainsworth observed. 'Any reason for me to remain, John? If not, I'll move homewards.'

'You'll be in tomorrow morning, sir?'

'Yes. And I have that conference with Dandruff Dan in the afternoon.'

'Three o'clock, sir.'

The gentleman referred to was the ancient chief clerk of an eminent firm of solicitors. He was a Dickensian figure who knew more of the practical aspects of the law than a good many qualified lawyers, and he was a generally welcome visitor in the Temple, apart from the liberal sprinkling of dandruff he always left behind as a memento of his visits. Edward, the junior clerk in Martin Ainsworth's chambers, had once suggested they should follow him about with a small dustpan and brush, but John had not been amused, and it had taken Edward several days to rehabilitate himself in his senior's estimation.

Ainsworth turned to go when John spoke. 'I don't think I yet know your long vacation plans, sir?'

'Because I don't know them myself. I shall probably go off somewhere around the middle of August and I'll let you know as soon as I've decided where. It'll possibly be to the top of a Swiss mountain. I must find some clean fresh air to breathe.'

'My wife and I found Norway very refreshing last year, sir,' John said, helpfully, though making the country sound rather like an iced drink.

'Where are you going this year?'

'Felixstowe. It's very bracing.'

'I'm sure it is. Well, good night, John.'

'Good night, sir.'

Martin Ainsworth lived in Knightsbridge, where he shared a pleasant and extremely comfortable flat with a maiden aunt who, though now in her seventies, managed to keep the years splendidly at bay. They each lived their own lives, had their own friends, and went their separate ways on holiday, but between them there existed a bond of respect and affection which was the stronger for not relying on any overt display of emotion.

The flat was empty when he arrived back, and he remembered that it was one of her bridge afternoons. That meant they would either go and dine together at one of the numerous new restaurants which had sprung up in the neighbourhood, or he could take himself off to his club and dine in masculine insularity.

Meanwhile, he fetched himself a Scotch on the rocks and settled down to read the evening paper, the front page of which carried an account of the closing stages of the trial, together with one of those feature articles written in advance but only published after a conviction. The present writer gave the impression that he'd spent the last few years living inside the secret radio transmitter which had been found beneath the garage floor of Crofton's Wimbledon home. Ainsworth read the piece with quizzical interest. It was skilfully written, and only the few with actual knowledge would be able to tell where fact petered out and imagination took over. In the middle of the article was a photograph of himself. He couldn't think where it had been taken and hoped he didn't often look like that. His mouth was open and his expression more or less vacant.

He heard a key in the front door, and a second or two later Aunt Virginia came in. She was a small, bird-like woman with subtly tinted iron-grey hair ('Nature's grey is like old fog and can you see me orange or blue?') and brisk movements. As usual she was dressed in expensive black. She threw her black crocodile bag on to a chair.

'A ghastly afternoon. I drew that dreadful woman who's a friend of May Thatcher, and she's cost me a small fortune with her obtuse bidding and wild doubling.'

'Why do you have her if she can't play?'

'Because May Thatcher asked us to; said she plays a respectable game.' Aunt Virginia raised her eyes to the ceiling and through it to heaven beyond. 'I've never known a woman have such a penchant for surrounding herself with lame ducks as May.'

'Have a drink?' Ainsworth said soothingly.

'I had one just before I left, but I'll have another. A gin and french.' She sat down at one end of the sofa and tucked her legs beneath her, having first kicked off her shoes. 'I'm sorry you didn't win your case, Martin; not that you expected to, did you?' He shook his head as he came across the room with her drink. 'May switched on the six o'clock news and we heard the result then. I was able to bask in reflected glory. My bridge friends are always very impressed by your forensic appearances.'

'So far they can afford to be. And what did they think about the sentence?'

'I think May Thatcher's friend was the only one to make any comment.'

'Which was?'

'She just said "poor man". I felt like asking her if she'd still have thought of him as a poor man when the Russians had taken over our country.'

'Bravo, Aunt.'

'All right, Martin, I know you think I'm a dyed-in-the-wool reactionary——'

'But you are.'

'Which I probably am, but there's too much wishy-washy sentimentality about crime these days. I'm not in favour of corporal punishment and strangely enough I have an open mind on hanging, but for heaven's sake let's vigorously enforce the laws we have still got before anarchy sets in for good.'

'A spy, the sort Crofton was, is in rather a different category from the ordinary run of criminal,' Ainsworth remarked mildly.

'I dare say, but that doesn't mean I have to love him any more than I do the tax inspector.' She unfolded her legs and stood up. 'What are we going to do about dinner, Martin? Are we going out or would you sooner I made an omelette or what?'

'Let's go out, Aunt.'

'All right, but not to that Spanish place. I don't want any more oily morsels served on to my lap.'

Over dinner they talked of books and plays and finally of summer holidays. 'Have you decided yet, when and where you're going, Martin?'

'No, but I will do in the next few days.'

'You don't have to, but Mrs. Carp will be going off for a fortnight in the middle of August, and I don't imagine you want to fend for yourself.'

'I can make my own bed and always eat out.'

'You know you can't sleep after you've made your bed three nights' running.'

'That's only happened once.'

'There's only been once.'

'How long are you going to be away?'

'About three weeks. A week in Scotland with Alison, a week with the Moores and finally my duty visit to Grace.'

Aunt Virginia's holidays always followed a pattern, visits to friends with comfortable country homes, followed inevitably by a duty visit to Grace, her widowed sister-in-law who lived in a small cottage on the edge of Exmoor. Martin suspected that each regarded the other as something of a chore to be borne once a year in the late summer.

'Oh, well, don't worry, I'll get out of the way, too.'

'You need a good break, you've had a busy term. Better to spend your earnings on a holiday now than on doctor's bills later. Why don't you go to America again? You've lots of invitations.'

'I'll think about it.'

But in fact, as invariably happens, Martin Ainsworth's mind was made up for him. It happened the next day.

He had been in chambers about an hour when the telephone rang and John announced rather mysteriously,

'A Mr. Green wishes to speak to you, sir. He says it's something private.' As though in reproof, he added, 'It's not either of the Mr. Greens we know.'

'Any idea what he wants?'

'No, sir, he declined to tell me. Shall I put him through?'

'I suppose you'd better.' There was a click as the connection was made. 'Martin Ainsworth speaking, who's that?'

'Green here, Ainsworth. The Attorney-General introduced us at court the other day. . . .'

'Yes, of course, I remember.' What he did remember was a short, sandy-haired man with a steady gaze and a strong handshake. He had learnt subsequently that Green was a very senior officer in the Security Service. Their actual meeting, however, had been fleeting and casual as Ainsworth made his way to the robing-room. Removing some of the frost from his tone, he now said, 'What can I do for you?'

'I'd be very grateful if I might send one of my fellows round to see you.'

'Certainly. May I ask, what about?'

'I'd sooner not discuss that over the 'phone.'

'Oh!'

'May I just say it's something arising out of the case we've each recently been interested in.'

'All right. What do you suggest?'

'If it suits you, I'll get Bowes—that's his name by the way, Robert Bowes—to call you and make an appointment.'

'Certainly. I'll be in chambers all day.'

11

'Many thanks. I'll tell him.'

After Green had rung off, Ainsworth summoned his clerk.

'A Mr. Bowes will be 'phoning me later, John. You can put him straight through.'

Bowes, however, didn't call till the afternoon, and then wasted few words.

'Could we meet this evening?' he asked after briskly introducing himself.

'All right,' Ainsworth replied without enthusiasm. 'Where?'

Bowes mentioned the name of a respectable but dowdy hotel in the Victoria area. 'Six o'clock in the main lounge. O.K.?'

'Yes. How shall I recognise you?'

'You don't need to, Mr. Ainsworth. I know *you*.'

2

It was between five and ten past six when Martin Ainsworth arrived at the hotel. Though normally a punctual person who, if anything, was early rather than late for his appointments, he regarded it as a matter of principle to keep Mr. Robert Bowes waiting a few minutes. There was something quietly and exasperatingly omniscient about these security boys. The velvet glove was invariably a bit too velvety, and the effect on the ordinary person was to evoke strong feelings of schoolboy rebellion. It was in some such mood that Ainsworth strode into the lobby of the hotel and cast a displeased look around him.

'Good evening, Mr. Ainsworth, it's good of you to come.'

Ainsworth turned sharply. The man must have been sitting over in a corner level with the door, from which vantage point he would spot anyone entering before they were likely to notice him. 'I'm Robert Bowes. There's a quiet spot the other side of the lounge if that's all right.'

Without waiting for a reply, he led the way across the room in which the last remains of post matinée teas were merging with the occasional medium sherry and small gin and tonic. For their rendezvous was a redoubt of respectable middle-aged ladies and of rather older men, who all resembled retired minor civil servants.

Ainsworth reckoned Bowes to be around forty. He had a lot of faintly golden-tinted fair hair, a reddish face and a small, bristly moustache which was undeniably ginger in effect. He couldn't be anything other than retired Army. Probably, Ainsworth guessed, a captain in one of the less snobby regiments. It seemed to him from what he had seen that our security gents largely fell into two groups. The ex-military like Bowes and the much younger, somewhat faceless young men who weren't long down from university. These were the field workers; the top executives like Green formed yet a third group. Between them, they doubtless accounted for all the required qualities.

'What can I order you? Gin? Sherry?' Bowes motioned him to take the more comfortable-looking of the two chairs.

'Scotch on the rocks, please.'

'The scotch'll probably be easier to get than the rocks. The British idea of ice in a drink is still one half-melted lump floating at the top of the glass. Anyway, let's see what we can do.

'I'm sorry I was so brief on the 'phone,' he went on, when the waiter had drifted away with their order, 'but that's one of the troubles with our job, we either can't say anything or when we do it's wrapped up in so much circumlocution you almost need a cypher clerk to interpret what we've said.' He smiled tentatively. It was a pleasant smile and revealed a row of small white teeth.

'Were you yourself connected with the Crofton case in any way?' Ainsworth asked, deciding the sooner they reached the point of the meeting, the better.

'Yes, only in the background, though. I'm not in the section which was responsible for his apprehension. I think you probably know we're pretty compartmentalised in our job. We take the view in this country that the less anyone knows what anyone else is doing in security, the better. It's a sound principle, though it can lead to the right hand being embarrassed by the left on occasions.' He gave Ainsworth another of his tentative smiles. Then taking a sip at his drink, he leaned forward and went on in an earnest tone, 'As you know, Crofton was a pretty big fish. But he was also a completely silent one, and we learnt nothing like as much from him as we hoped for, which means that the network he operated remains intact.' He fixed Ainsworth with a steady gaze. 'We're wondering whether perhaps he may have let fall something in your presence which would give us a line to follow up. I believe you had a number of interviews with him.'

The words ceased, but the steady gaze continued as Martin Ainsworth considered what he should say.

'I don't think you have any right to ask me that,' he said at length. 'After all, Crofton was my professional client and what passed between us was under the seal of professional confidence.'

'I appreciate that, Mr. Ainsworth, but wasn't it the Lord Chief Justice himself who said that matters affecting national security had prior demands over individual rights and privileges. Anyway, something to that effect. But perhaps I can help you by asking a direct question. Did Crofton at any time ever mention the name of any associate?'

'Well, that I can answer and with a "no".'

'He never mentioned anyone in Germany or anyone with a German name?'

'Never. You said just now that he was a silent fish and I can confirm that. In all the conversations I had with him, he never once said anything which could be of possible significance to you and yours. With one exception, he never alluded to his past or made any admissions about what he was. As you're aware, his defence was simply that he *was* a genuine British business man. When all the evidence pointed otherwise, he just maintained an attitude of stolid impassivity. In the face of overwhelming proof, he admitted nothing. *Nothing.*'

'With one exception, you said,' Bowes said keenly.

'When I went to see him immediately after he'd been sentenced, he let drop some remark to the effect, "We only gave Greville Wynne eight years".'

'We?'

'Just so.'

'And that's all?'

'That's all.' Ainsworth drained his glass and looked ostentatiously at his watch. The next moment, however, he felt as if an electric charge had riven his body.

'I was hoping you might have heard him mention the name Seidler. Elli Seidler,' Bowes's tone had suddenly become more compelling. 'I can see that the name is known to you.'

It seemed to Martin Ainsworth that several years passed before he responded. Certainly in the few seconds before he did speak, events of twenty-five years ago had stormed the present out of his mind.

'Yes,' he said slowly. 'I once knew someone called Elli Seidler. In Berlin before the war.'

'She still lives there,' Bowes said with the air of a doctor imparting some functional piece of news to his patient.

'I haven't been in touch with her.'

'But you used to know her extremely well, I believe. This may sound a trifle impertinent, but I'm also told you once wanted to marry her.'

Ainsworth looked up angrily. 'Someone seems to have been very busy with my past. Perhaps you'd tell me why and what the hell any of this has to do with the Crofton case.' All his earlier rancour about the security forces and their minions returned in a hot blast. It was insufferable that they should have been secretly turning over his earlier life—and getting so much of it right. Then he remembered that before he had been allowed access to any of the more secret material in the Crofton case, some fellow had come along to chambers one morning and given him a vetting. He had asked a great number of questions and passed a few cautionary strictures and departed. Presumably he had then gone away and, starting with his registration of birth in Somerset House, laboriously worked his way forward year by year to Martin Ainsworth of current habits and tastes.

'I really do apologise for being so disconcerting,' Bowes said disarmingly, 'but I now come to the real guts of our meeting. Before I do so, however, I must stress the necessity for complete secrecy in respect of what I'm about to tell you. One of our chaps has seen you, I believe, and, so to speak, given you the standard shot in the arm.

'Elli Seidler runs a language school in Dahlem, a suburb of Berlin in the American sector. But that is only a front for her main activities. She's on the pay roll of the East German Intelligence Service. In other words she's a Communist spy, and an extremely astute one at that.'

He paused as if to let the full import of his words sink in.

'But you seem to know all about her, nevertheless,' Ainsworth observed.

'We've only recently uncovered her.'

'What's this got to do with me?'

'Are you surprised to hear that she's a Communist spy?'

'When one hasn't seen somebody for twenty-five years, one isn't necessarily surprised to hear anything about them. And the past twenty-five years have wrought dramatic changes in a good many lives.' He paused and looked thoughtful a moment. 'No, I'm not wholly surprised. As you doubtless know,' his tone was gently ironic, 'she was always violently anti-Nazi and her husband Wolfgang died in a concentration camp a few months before the war began. That was after I had returned to England and it was then I suggested we should get married. But we didn't, and the war came and I've not been in touch with her since. I didn't even know if she was still alive. I take it she has re-married?'

· 'No, and the only photograph of a male in her house is one of you. It stands in a silver frame on a small table in the living-room.'

For a full minute, Ainsworth could only stare into his empty glass. His mind was now so flooded with memories of Elli it seemed impossible that it was less than twenty minutes ago he had entered the hotel and met Bowes for the first time. It had taken this stranger to unseat his mental poise and fill him with thoughts which belonged to a part of his life he had firmly believed to be locked away in the cupboard for ever. Above all, he felt a gnawing desire to know more.

Bowes went on, 'And now the proposition, Mr. Ainsworth. We're asking you to go to Berlin and resume touch with Elli Seidler.'

'Why?' He knew the answer but felt the necessity to stall.

'We would like you to try and penetrate her organisation. In fact'—he made a small, self-deprecating gesture with his mouth —'we want you to do a job of intelligence for us. Let me explain further. We're pretty certain that Elli Seidler was in some way tied in with Crofton, though so far we've not been able to find out how. She is, as I've said, an extremely astute operator, and though she'd been at it for years, we were only recently successful in uncovering her. You're probably wondering why we've not pulled her in. Well, the answer is, if you haven't already guessed, that we hope to learn a little more before we do so. That is, if you will help us. What we are most anxious to discover is her means of communication with her own side. It's not secret radios or anything of that nature. There's a courier service of some sort. We want to know who's in it and how it operates.'

'And what on earth makes you think I should be successful in finding out?'

'Maybe you won't. That's a risk we're prepared to take. But there's a chance that someone out of Frau Seidler's past will succeed where present associates fail. Provided that someone is you. The silver-framed photograph, remember. You must still be very much in her thoughts for that to be retained in a place of honour.'

There was a silence. Then Ainsworth said, 'Apart from anything else, it's a thoroughly despicable thing you're asking me to do.

'Despicable? Is safeguarding your country's security despicable? I'm sorry if I've not made myself clear. We're not asking you to undertake a splendid romantic adventure. Espionage and counter-espionage are jobs like any other. Dull, full of routine, much more so than the public ever imagines, and from time to time a certain degree squalid. After all, I don't imagine you're still in love with the woman or you'd have done something about it before now. In police states, children are taught to spy on parents, servants on employers, janitors on residents and so on. Well, we don't practise that here as an article of faith, but we're not beyond suggesting that a man should try and worm his way back into the confidence of a woman with whom he had an affair twenty-five years before.' He gave the lounge a raking look. 'All expenses paid, of course,' he added, as though this might otherwise be a stumbling block.

'I take it I may have time to think?'

'Certainly, but if you could let me know tomorrow, please.'

'And if I agree, when would you suggest my leaving?'

'As soon as possible. Today's Thursday; say, at the weekend.'

'That's absurd.'

Bowes shrugged. 'Of course if you have commitments . . . but I understood the long vacation was starting in a few days' time.'

'It is.'

'Well then?'

'I must think it over. You don't seem to realise it, but in the course of one short half-hour you've spun me, pummelled me and thrown me against the ropes, and now you're casually suggesting I should abruptly change the course of my life for you.'

Bowes laughed good-naturedly. 'I apologise again. I'm afraid we get used to ours running like fork-lightning, we're apt to forget that other people often spend theirs nestling in comfortable ruts. Not that I'm suggesting you do.'

'I nestle in an extremely comfortable rut, as a matter of fact. However. . . . How do I get in touch with you?'

Bowes scribbled a telephone number on a piece of paper and passed it over. 'Call me there, and if you're willing to help, perhaps we could meet and discuss actual details.' He gave the lounge a distasteful glance. 'I'd be delighted if you'd lunch with me. I won't subject you to this place again.'

'There is just one further point,' Ainsworth said, in a tone which caused Bowes to watch him attentively. 'How do I know you're what you pretend to be? You've . . .'

Bowes broke in impatiently. 'Good grief, this isn't April Fool's

Day.' He fished inside a pocket and produced a card in a plastic case for Ainsworth's inspection. 'This satisfy you?'

It bore a recognisable photograph, the name 'Robert Andrew Bowes', an indecipherable signature above the designation 'Under-Secretary of State', and a Foreign Office stamp.

'Of course you're a lawyer,' Bowes said with a grin, putting the card away again, 'and everything must be proved beyond reasonable doubt. I'm sorry, I ought to have shown that to you at the beginning, but producing it always makes me feel like a policeman about to arrest somebody. And anyway I thought Charles Green had vouched for me.'

They walked across to the main door and out on to the pavement where Bowes held out his hand. 'I'll look forward to hearing from you tomorrow.' He lowered his voice and went on with the utmost seriousness, 'Meanwhile, may I impress on you again not to repeat a word of this to anyone—not even to your aunt.'

Before Martin Ainsworth could think of a suitable retort, he had strode away in the direction of Victoria Station. A cab drew up to disgorge some passengers and Ainsworth gratefully seized it. He decided to go to his club, have a quiet drink and sort out his thoughts.

For a time, though, his mind remained focused immovably on the past, on the year 1935, which he had spent as a student in Berlin, living at the Pension Seidler near the Tiergarten and going off each morning to the University in Unter den Linden. Wolfgang and Elli Seidler had not been much older than the dozen or so students who lodged with them, and the high point of the day, he remembered, was the evening meal when they all came together and the air would become thick with the exchange of opinions, proffered and hurled in as many accents as there were people present. There was a blond Swedish boy who spoke excellent German and who used to argue the virtues of Hitlerism. Jean-Pierre, a sallow, dark-eyed French lad with a mercurial expression, invariably led the counter-attack with Gallic thrust and enjoyment. Then there was Herzi, a Swiss dumpling of a girl who was interested in infant welfare but who reacted vigorously when Stefan, an amorous Hungarian, misread the signs and attempted to seduce her.

But above all, he remembered Elli and Wolfgang presiding over the table each evening, listening and joining in. Elli's main contribution was simply to help out those whose views were throttled by problems of language, and tactfully to correct others who were emasculating her native tongue beyond permissible limits.

Wolfgang made no great secret of his anti-Nazi views, and Martin had known that he spent a good deal of his time attending meetings of like-minded people, though he had no knowledge of their precise purpose or of what transpired. One of the Seidlers' closest friends, an ascetic-looking young man with deep-sunk eyes, whose name Martin couldn't now remember, often used to come to supper, and then he and Wolfgang would invariably go off together afterwards to attend some meeting or another.

From the start Martin had been one of Elli's favourites. She was only a year older than himself and professed a love of all Englishmen, and for most of the time he was the only one staying at the pension. Though she spoke reasonable English, she always insisted that they converse in German. But after that grimly frightening day when Wolfgang failed to come home from a meeting and they subsequently heard he had been arrested, everything changed. They not only spoke English together but their whole relationship experienced a cathartic jolt. That had been about two months before Martin had been due to return to England, and during that remaining period he did all that a rather callow young man could have done to help and sustain her. She appeared to have no one else she preferred to lean on and he, for his part, did more than enough to justify her love of a particular Englishman. It was in the last week of his stay that she had asked him for a photograph and he had gone off and had a huge one taken. It embarrassed him now to think how vulgarly large it was. Embarrassment, however, tinged with intrigue that it still existed, and in a silver frame, too.

After his return to England—a return he would most certainly have put off but for parental injunction—he kept in touch with her by almost daily letter and then, when, a few months before the outbreak of war, he heard that Wolfgang had died in a concentration camp, he wrote asking her to come to England with a view to becoming his bride. If she would say 'yes' he would arrive on the first plane to fetch her. But she hadn't said 'yes'; she had said she wanted time to think, she was still bruised and dazed by recent events. Nevertheless, she loved him more than anyone and asked to see him again. And then the war had come and all ties were severed overnight. By the time it ended, Martin Ainsworth, like everyone else, was six years older in age and considerably more so in worldly experience. Blonde, slightly plump Elli, with her bright, friendly eyes and her soft, firm skin, was confined, with other youthful memories, to a top shelf in his mind, to be taken down and examined at decreasing intervals, and never with any serious intent of further action.

And yet now that was precisely what he was being asked to take. For Queen and country, moreover. The whole notion was fantastic; also, as he had said to Bowes, thoroughly disagreeable. Where did one's loyalties lie in such a situation? One thing was certain, Elli's professed love of Englishmen hadn't prevented *hers* from being devoted to causes now working against his own country.

The cab pulled up and Ainsworth entered his club.

'Hello there, Ainsworth.' A voice hailed him from the staircase. He looked round to see Mr. Justice Penrey.

'Good evening, Judge.'

'Come on up to the bar and let me buy you a drink.'

With a silent sigh, he fell in step beside the judge and mounted the stairs.

'Hope you didn't think I was too harsh on that fellow of yours?' Mr. Justice Penrey said, puffing slightly. 'But what else can one do as the world is today?'

'Difficult, certainly.'

'I thought he comported himself with considerable dignity. He'd have made a good golfer with that pair of shoulders he was continually bracing. Pity they don't play the game in Russia.'

'He was a member of South Bucks Club and played there.'

Mr. Justice Penrey let out a guffaw of laughter.

'Of course, these spy trials are like icebergs. Six-sevenths of what has gone on remains out of sight. You and I and the jury are only told as much as is needful to administer justice, but I'd dearly like to know some of the rest. For example, a string of people must be feeling uneasy as a result of Crofton's arrest. Whole elaborate networks may have to be dismantled and even abandoned, and fresh ones put together piece by piece. That's something you and I and the public never get to know about. It fascinates me. Perhaps I've missed my vocation. As it is, I have to make do with spy stories. I'm a great reader of them—the decently-written ones, mind you—though it seems to be one of the realms where truth really is stranger than fiction.' They reached the bar. 'What's it going to be?'

Ainsworth smiled as he said, 'I think, as a token of respect to my recent client, I should have vodka and something. That should go for you, too, Judge.'

'Two vodka martinis then.' When the drinks arrived, Mr. Justice Penrey raised his glass. 'Here's damnation to all spies coupled with the hope you'll have a pleasant long vacation.'

The next morning Ainsworth called the Victoria number and asked for Bowes. When he recognised his voice on the line, he simply said, 'I'm ready to have lunch with you.'

3

It was not a sense of patriotic duty that drove him to make the appointment. At least, certainly not a conscious one, though, looking back afterwards, he was pleased to believe that it had had its motivating effect. Uppermost, however, was the appeal to masculine vanity, and the novelty of the challenge; and, furthermore, acceptance meant a break with routine. Like a good many men whose lives have settled into comfortable ruts, Martin Ainsworth was sometimes bothered by introspective reflections on the inadequate aims of his existence. If the reflections happened to fall on a Sunday, then he would put an additional coin in the collecting plate, but otherwise they usually died away by the next morning. One final factor in his mind was the utterly intriguing prospect of seeing Elli again, though this stirred no emotional chords within him. If it had, he would most probably have refused the assignment.

'Well, let's get down to discussing details,' Bowes said, drawing his coffee in front of him. This time their rendezvous was a Soho restaurant where they had just finished an excellent lunch. The one similarity between this and their previous meeting was the discreet corner table, and Ainsworth had come to assume that agoraphobia was one of the phobias with which members of the Security Services were injected early on in their training. He wondered if they broke out into pink rashes if left for long in the middle of rooms. 'The first thing, of course,' Bowes went on, 'is the reason you give her for suddenly appearing out of the blue—and here the important point is not to tell her anything which can be proved false. However, there's no difficulty about this in your case; you spent a year in Berlin as a student and now you've returned to see the city again. Incidentally, you'll probably be surprised at the number of tourists you do find there. Not so many Europeans, but it's become quite a pilgrim centre for Americans and Asians. After all, it has all the morbid fascination of the trigger mechanism of a nuclear bomb. And having come to Berlin, what more natural than to look for her name in the telephone book and——'

'What is her address, incidentally?'

'Karolinerstrasse, 14, in Dahlem.' He fetched a small, black-covered notebook from his pocket, tore out a page and wrote down the address, followed by a telephone number. 'It's a small villa with about a quarter of an acre of garden in a wooded area. It's within comfortable walking distance of Dahlem Dorf underground station.'

'You seem to know all about it.'

'I've not seen the house myself, but I do know all about it, inside as well as out,' Bowes said.

'And after I've made my first courtesy call, what do I do next?'

'Follow it up by inviting her out to dinner. Date her as much as you can. The whole scheme rests on your insinuating your-self back into her confidence. Chat about old times, relive the past together and then see what you can find out about the present.' He observed Ainsworth's distinctly dubious expression and went on, 'If this all sounds rather dreamlike, let me assure you of one thing which is the common experience of everyone in my line of business, and it'd be borne out by any psychologist you cared to mention it to. Every man, woman and child on this earth has hidden somewhere in the recesses of their conscious mind a button. Find that button and press it and you won't be able to stem the flood of words. And by words, I mean confession. It's all a question of finding the button. It may take days, weeks, months, it may take only hours or minutes, but everybody has one built into their character somewhere.'

'What about Crofton? Nobody seems to have been able to find his button.'

'But he's got one,' Bowes said forthrightly.

'And you think I may be able to get Elli Seidler to talk about the present by digging over the past?'

'I think you stand a better chance than anyone of helping her unburden her mind.' He paused. 'After the initial meeting you'll have to play it largely by ear. That's what you frequently have to do in court, isn't it? It'll be a matter of adjusting your tactics as you go along.'

'Will one of your chaps be in touch with me in Berlin?'

'Yes, a man named Lander. He'll meet you and look after your needs throughout your stay. Incidentally, do you know anyone at all in Berlin?'

Ainsworth shook his head.

'Good,' Bowes said, 'because we wouldn't want you to get in touch with friends or anything like that. As far as we're concerned, no one is to know of your presence, not even the British Commandant. Just one or two of our own people. Lander will give you further details when you arrive.'

'Where shall I be staying?'

'Hotel Lübeck, just off the Uhlandstrasse and a few minutes' walk from the Kurfürstendamm. It's small and quiet, but I think you'll find it comfortable.'

From Bowes's tone, Ainsworth had a vision of the Hotel Lübeck staffed by secret agents and wired to record every snore. He would have preferred to have stayed at one of the large hotels—the Bristol Kempinski and the Hilton were the two main ones in West Berlin, he understood—but he realised that Bowes would not have countenanced such a suggestion.

'And you'll be ready to fly on Monday?'

'If that's what you want.'

'There's a 'plane which gets you to Berlin around lunchtime, with a single put down at Cologne. We'll book you on that and inform Lander.'

'First class, I hope.'

'It's a tourist-only flight, I'm afraid,' Bowes said complacently.

'Supposing I want to get in touch with you over the weekend?'

'You have my number.'

'Surely you don't spend the whole of Saturday and Sunday in your office.'

'There's always a duty officer, and this weekend it happens to be me,' Bowes replied, with a rueful grin. 'Anything else, Mr. Ainsworth?'

'Not that I can think of, but I'll call you should it be necessary.'

'Well, I'll say goodbye till Monday morning. I'll pick you up at your flat at eight-thirty and drive you out to the airport. Don't forget your passport. I'll have your ticket.' They were about to get up from the table when he added, 'By the way, have you thought how you're going to explain the trip to your aunt?' He mentioned her as naturally as if she was their common acquaintance.

'I'll just say I have an urge to go and see Berlin again.'

'Yes,' Bowes said slowly, and added with a faint note of

asperity, 'though I hope you'll make it sound rather more convincing than you did then.'

Happily, Ainsworth didn't have to break the news to Aunt Virginia until bedtime, as she was out when he returned home, and was going straight on, he remembered, to dinner and a theatre. It was eleven o'clock before she came in.

'Enjoy the play?' he asked, though her expression clearly revealed what her view of it had been.

'Ghastly! A lot of promiscuous young people in a sort of bombed-out temple, which was supposed to be near Huddersfield of all places. I never thought I'd live to say it, but I'd sooner have seen one of those tinkling musicals your father so used to enjoy.'

'Did Hester enjoy it?'

'She said she did,' Aunt Virginia retorted scornfully. 'But she would never admit not enjoying anything in the fashion of the moment. For an intelligent woman, her attitude surprises me.'

'Well, now I'll surprise you, aunt,' Ainsworth said with a faintly mischievous smile. 'I'm going to Berlin on Monday.'

'Berlin!' Aunt Virginia exclaimed, as though he might have said Vladivostok or Chungking. 'What in heaven's name is taking you to Berlin?'

'I've had it at the back of my mind for some while that I'd like to see it again, and I happened to meet someone the other day who'd just returned from there and who fired my imagination to revisit the city.'

'But you were only saying a few days ago that you hadn't decided where to go this year.'

'I know. I made my mind up on the spur of the moment. I'll spend about a week there and then probably go down to the Bavarian Alps.'

'Do you still know anyone in Berlin?' Aunt Virginia asked suspiciously.

'Not that I'm aware of.'

'What was the name of that girl you used to correspond with?'

'Elli Seidler, do you mean?'

'Yes, what's become of her?'

'Heaven knows! As far as I was concerned, she fell from sight with the war.'

'I suppose it will be quite interesting to see it again,' Aunt Virginia conceded thoughtfully. 'You won't go nosing around in the Communist part, will you?'

'I may do; depends. I understand there are official sightseeing tours into East Berlin.'

His aunt pursed her lips. 'Well, all I can say is be careful. One's always reading of people having difficulties with those young border sentries.' She paused. 'And you are going on Monday, did you say?'

He nodded. 'Having made up my mind, I thought I'd better get out of the flat before you do. Then you and Mrs. Carp can cast your dust sheets without hindrance.'

As he spoke, he was surprised to find that, having reached his decision, he was not beset by any second thoughts as to its wisdom. He didn't even give Bowes a further call, and was ready, packed and waiting, when he arrived outside the flat punctually at eight-thirty on Monday morning.

'Did your aunt accept your explanation?' Bowes asked, with more than polite interest, as they began the drive out to the airport.

'Naturally,' Ainsworth replied. He had no intention of entering into a discussion of the subject, and resented the constant treatment as a child. Any minute Bowes would be asking if he'd remembered to clean his teeth and pack his crayons.

'What have you told your chambers?'

'That I'm going to Berlin,' he said, in as blighting a tone as he could manage.

'For a holiday?'

'Precisely.'

'And is there anyone else who knows your plans?'

'One more question in this series,' Ainsworth exploded, 'and I'll have it announced over the public address system of London Airport exactly why Martin Ainsworth *is* going to Berlin.'

'I'm sorry,' Bowes said in an apparently chastened mood. 'It's habit again. But if you knew just how insecure we are as a race, you'd understand.'

'You may be able to speak for the rest of the nation,' Ainsworth retorted stuffily, 'but please don't assume I have to be told everything ten times over.'

He was not a normally arrogant person, and almost immediately afterwards felt rather ashamed of his peevish outburst.

The rest of the journey passed in silence and it was a relief when they arrived.

It was a further relief when he was able to pass through immigration control and leave Bowes behind. It occurred to him later that, but for his display of petulance, Bowes would most likely have used his pass to accompany him right to the foot of the aircraft boarding-steps. As it was, they got through their farewells in the main hall of the building.

'I wish you every success on your assignment, Mr. Ainsworth,' Bowes had said solemnly, grasping his hand.

'Don't expect too much, that's all. I'm not a professional at the game, remember.'

And now his flight number was being called. As he joined a stream of other passengers trailing the blue light, he reflected that the point of no return had just been passed.

4

MARTIN AINSWORTH had not been in Germany since before the war, if one didn't count a number of visits to the British zone in the immediate post-war years to participate at courts martial. However, he'd no sooner set foot inside the Cologne Airport building than he knew he was back. There was the unmistakable smell of cigar and fried food that he always associated with German restaurants.

Forty-five minutes later, he was airborne again and heading east. The majority of his fellow passengers were now Germans who had joined the 'plane at Cologne. There had been some touching farewells between members of families who lived with a hundred miles of hated East Germany separating them.

They hadn't been flying long when the 'plane began to weave and lose height. Shortly afterwards the captain's voice came over the wire.

'Ladies and gentlemen, we are about to enter the corridor down which we shall fly to Berlin at a height of nine thousand feet.'

Nine thousand feet! It seemed to Ainsworth they were almost skimming the tree-tops compared with their previous height. He gazed out with rapt interest at a landscape which was disappointingly similar to what it had been before the announcement. He smiled to himself and wondered what he had expected to see. Ogres wearing goatee beards trying frantically to snatch the 'plane out of the air?

What was apparent after a time was the emptiness of the roads and the absence of any signs of life in the few villages over which they passed. Then with a sudden tingle of excitement, he recognised the lakes which bounded Berlin on its west and south-west sides, and a few minutes later they were over Berlin itself, looking in all its spaciousness like a garden city. How grateful the West Berliners must be, he reflected, for that air of spaciousness.

Before he had time to identify any further landmarks, the wheels caught the runway of Tempelhof Airport and they were taxi-ing up to the apron, the only one Ainsworth knew of where you actually disembarked under cover. It was like running straight into the hangar.

He followed the herd into the vast new hall and waited for his bags. The one thing which never seemed to get speeded up in air travel was the unloading of baggage. It remained attuned to the days of huge, lumbering bi-planes which heaved and rattled across the frontiers of Europe at a bumpy 120 miles-per-hour.

'Mr. Ainsworth?' He turned at the sound of his name to find a small, neat man with a broad head and carefully-brushed dark hair standing beside him. The man's expression was pleasant but in a completely neutral way. 'My name's Stephen Lander, let me help you with your bags. I have the car outside.'

His English, though perfect, bore a distant trace of accent. Ainsworth decided he was of central European origin and had most probably learnt his English in America. As an intelligence agent he would certainly have the merit of moving unobtrusively in any company.

They reached the car, an Opel, and Lander showed all the assiduity of a hotel commissionaire in holding open the door for Ainsworth and then in stowing away his two suitcases.

'You'll find Berlin a very different place from when you were last here,' he remarked agreeably as they drove off.

'No doubt.'

From now on, Ainsworth decided he would assume that everyone he met from Bowes's mob knew every detail of his life, past and present. If he could bring himself to accept this, he wouldn't feel nettled each time an apparent stranger revealed possession of such knowledge.

'Well, Mr. Lander, I'm now in your hands,' he said. 'What's first on the agenda?'

'I suggest you make your first contact with Elli this evening.'

'This evening!' His tone echoed dismay. Somehow he'd expected he would be given a day or two to become acclimatised. This was as bad as the business executive who is whisked from 'plane to conference and then back again to fly on to the next continent.

'She is always at home and alone on Monday evenings,' Lander said, as though describing the habits of an ornithological species, 'so it will be an excellent opportunity for you to call on her. If you arrive about eight-thirty, she will have finished her supper, and you'll have all the advantage of surprise.'

'And have *you* any bright ideas of how I should set about things when I get there?'

'Elli is a lonely woman and a nervous one. Spying is a hazardous operation, especially when you're operating in hostile territory and more especially still in Berlin. The city is possibly a little less spy-ridden than it was a few years ago when every other person on the street was somebody's agent and the whole profession got a very bad name'—his tone was cynically detached—'but scarcely a week goes by without some mysterious disappearance or another in the cause of espionage. If Elli knew we were on to her, she'd be back through the wall in less time than it takes a frightened rabbit to bolt down its hole. Even so, she must guess it's only a matter of time. You've been her saviour once before, if that doesn't describe it too dramatically; there's a chance she'll see you in the same rôle again. Keep your eyes and ears well open, Mr. Ainsworth.'

'Shall I express sympathy with her side, pretend I'm a so-called woolly liberal when it comes to Communism?'

'No, I don't advise that line,' Lander said emphatically. 'It might put her on guard. Remember she's a seasoned agent and will be immediately suspicious of any unsubtle approach. No, definitely don't pretend you're a sympathiser.' He threw Ainsworth a conspiratorial smile. 'Above all, keep the main object of the exercise in mind, namely to discover her links with her East German masters.' His tone became grimly serious. 'It's very important that we should have that information—and soon.'

Ainsworth knew better than to probe that statement. In accordance with normal intelligence practice he had been told no more than was necessary to him in fulfilling the assignment. Elli was one end of a channel of communication: he was being asked to try and unearth the wires. What passed along them was not his concern. Sufficient that it was material damaging to the interests of his country.

His first view of the Hotel Lübeck was not encouraging. A child was being sick on the pavement immediately outside the entrance. It proved to be one of those establishments which exist entirely on upper floors apart from a small entrance lobby over which there now presided a prim-looking female in black bombazine. To complete the picture, her hair was parted in the middle and she actually wore pince-nez. Her manner was formally polite as she handed Ainsworth a registration form to complete and asked for his passport. He noticed that her skin had the colour and smoothness of candle wax. She could have been a governess under the Weimar Republic who had been washed forward in time, intact.

'I'll leave you to unpack,' Lander said, 'and'll call round just before eight o'clock. Dinner's at seven.' He gave the formidable female a small bow. 'Aufwiedersehen, Fräulein Grimmer.'

'Aufwiedersehen, Herr Lander.' It fascinated Ainsworth the way she appeared to unfold and refold her lips each time speech was required of her.

'Leave your bags here, Herr Ainsworth. The porter will bring them and I will show you to your room.'

'You speak excellent English, Fräulein,' Ainsworth said.

She nodded her acknowledgment of the compliment, but offered no explanation. Chumminess was obviously not encouraged, he reflected as he followed her upstairs.

'This is the lounge.' She indicated an empty room which reminded Ainsworth of every bourgeois German drawing-room he'd ever entered during his student days in the country. The blinds were half-drawn, the chairs looked unyielding. There were some hideous pieces of china on every available flat surface, and the air smelt as though it had been bottled in an earlier century and released for his arrival.

'Very nice,' he murmured.

'And this is the dining-room,' she said, waving a stately arm through the next doorway. 'Breakfast is from 8 to 9. Lunch from 12.30 to 1.30, and dinner,' she added firmly, 'is at 7. And now I will show you your room. It is one of our best.'

Through the door of the dining-room, Ainsworth had seen about eight tables, only half of them apparently in use. An untidy-looking girl was removing dishes from the remainder.

'How many guests does the hotel hold?' he asked politely, as he followed Fräulein Grimmer down a dingy corridor.

'Fifteen. We emphasise comfort rather than numbers,' she replied in a tone which seemed to reprove him for asking the question. 'And this is your room.' As she spoke, she unlocked the end door and stood aside for him to enter.

It was neither large nor elaborately furnished, but it required only a glance to see that it was spotlessly clean and perfectly comfortable. There were two chairs, a bedside light, and on the bed one of those enormous eiderdown affairs that resemble inflated rubber rafts. He was about to comment on the absence of washing facilities, when she threw open a door on the far side of the room. 'Here, your bathroom.'

This was an unexpected pleasure as it hadn't given the appearance of being the sort of establishment to provide private bathrooms. The bath was huge and, together with a water closet on a dais looking rather like a bishop's throne, occupied at least three-quarters of the floor space.

By the time he turned back into the bedroom, Fräulein Grimmer had silently departed. He walked across to the window, and discovered it looked out on to a small yard in which grew a chestnut tree. It had an air of calm and seclusion, and his initial misgivings began to melt away. Now that he was here, he would not only make the best of it, but could begin to feel that it was really a much more appropriate setting for recapturing the spirit of the place, than one of the big international-type hotels would have been.

There was a knock on the door, and an old man wearing a green apron staggered in with his two bags. He looked a cowed old boy and Ainsworth was scarcely surprised. He thanked him, and tipped him, and then set about unpacking. It was while he was doing so that he realised, with a pleasurable shock, that he had quite naturally slipped into German in his brief exchange with the porter.

By the time he had finished and had a wash, it was after three o'clock. Four hours to dinner, five to his meeting with Lander. 'Afternoon free' as the tour itineraries say, after having run their customers into the ground for several days on end.

Eager with anticipation, he set out to explore.

5

THE afternoon was close with a distant rumble of thunder to provide a proper Wagnerian salute to the returned visitor.

As he strolled down the Kurfürstendamm, the main thoroughfare of West Berlin, Ainsworth reflected that it was a long time since he'd seen so many pertly attractive girls and all very much dressed to take the male eye. Fräulein Grimmer would have looked as much out of place in this setting as a Victorian commode in a contemporary bathroom. As he approached the end of the street, the cafés and cinemas multiplied. It could have been the Champs Elysées blended with Hollywood Boulevard. He paused to study the efforts of young pavement artists, several of whom rivalled the great Italian masters when it came to the physical size of their composition. Indeed, one bearded youth's work disappeared beneath a table at which a large female sat tucking into chocolate cake.

Moving slowly through the crowd ahead of him was a bent old man with an enormous eagle on his gauntleted wrist. From time to time the old man stopped to rest and the bird would give its wings a half-hearted flap. Ainsworth was to see him on a number of further occasions, but never learnt where he was bound from or for. He and his huge predatory companion might, for all he knew, have no existence outside that quarter mile of smart, sophisticated street.

He arrived at the Kaiser Wilhelm Memorial Church, now rebuilt to resemble a gift-wrapped powder-puff and lipstick, with part of the burnt-out remains squeezed incongruously in the middle.

As he walked on in the direction of the Tiergarten, the scene began to change, to become more open. Indeed as he strode across what might have been a large open common, he realised with a sudden shock that this had been the area in which the Pension Seidler had been situated. Now it was acres of weeds and thistles interlaced by roads. He reached for the plan he had brought with him to get his bearings. Yes, the next turning on the right should be the street in which he had lived. He could see it from where he stood. Not a very long street but he was able to survey its whole length. Of the two dozen houses on each of its sides, not one brick remained. He gazed about him stunned. That this had been a thickly-populated and fashionable residential area! It was unbelievable. It was as though he were standing in Cromwell Road and not a building stood between him and Kensington Gardens.

He quickened his pace to reach the Tiergarten and lose himself amongst its deep, shady paths, though it, too, had been denuded of much of its foliage in the course of fighting. A notice informed him that British gifts had been largely responsible for its rehabilitation. How characteristic of his country to help its conquered enemy restore its parks and gardens.

On a Monday afternoon there were few people about and he strolled with pleasure in the vague direction of the Brandenburg Gate, the emotional talisman for all Berliners, though now just inside the eastern sector.

And suddenly, as he broke from the cover of the trees, there it was, just as he remembered it, until his glance moved lower and he saw the great buttressing semicircle of wall. At this distance, there was nothing particularly sinister about it. It might merely have been indicating a road diversion while new drains were laid.

He found himself opposite the Soviet War Memorial, which, with the innocence of that time, had been built inside the British sector of the city. Two Russian sentries stood on guard on the steps of the memorial round which ran a formidable wire fence. Outside the fence, British sentries patrolled. It seemed to Martin Ainsworth as he took in the scene that it crystallised as graphically as anything could the current world situation.

He walked on towards the wall and mounted an observation platform which stood only a few yards back from it. A young armed Vopo stood on a similar platform on his side of the wall. They might have been at opposite ends of a tennis court about to start play, and Ainsworth was struck by the utter absurdity of the situation. If it wasn't so grotesquely inhuman, it would be laughable.

Over against the arches of the great Gate other sentries in olive-green uniforms moved around. Farther back, down Unter den Linden, he could see a barrier which was clearly as close as East Berliners were allowed to approach. Occasionally people paused by the barrier and gazed in his direction, but never for very long. Buses and trams crossed his line of vision as he stood experiencing the strangest mixture of emotions which had ever gripped his mind. It was the complete unreality, even improbability, of the scene which sent his imagination reeling in a punch-drunk daze.

He became suddenly aware that the young Vopo was studying him through a pair of gigantic field-glasses, and he had an almost irresistible urge to pull faces.

Instead, however, he stared with calm deliberation over the young man's head.

About a mile and a half away, in the general line of Ainsworth's vision, in an office of the East German government, a man stretched out his hand to answer the telephone.

'Fröhlich,' he announced, and then a second or two later, 'Yes, I'll come at once, Comrade Grossman.'

He left his desk and made his way to the floor above. Outside a pair of imposing double doors, he paused and patted vaguely at the few strands of over-long hair which was all that now remained on the top of his head. His eyes lay deep in their sockets, but burnt with a fervour not reflected in the rest of his features which bore a generally worn air.

He knocked on the door and entered.

'Yes, Comrade Grossman, you wished to speak to me.'

Comrade Erika Grossman sat at a large desk, which befitted her senior rank. Moreover, the framed photographs of Lenin and Walter Ulbricht, who stared at each other from opposite walls, were grander than those which adorned his room. Hers was of Ulbricht the firm and spuriously benign leader. His was of an Ulbricht who looked as though his underclothing was chafing him. Their two Lenins, however, were the same pose, only his was smaller.

Erika Grossman was wearing her customary white blouse and dark-blue coat and skirt. She was a well-busted woman with blonde hair streaked with grey, which she took very little trouble with. Not for her mere lip-service in condemnation of the decadent ways of women in the countries of the Western world.

'Sit down, Hans,' she said genially. 'I called you because the

Minister is becoming restive at the lack of results in Dahlem. He thinks we should be getting on faster than we are. Quick results are imperative.'

Fröhlich shook his head in a gesture of impatience. 'With all respect to the comrade minister, I don't think we have done too badly . . .'

'Do I have to remind you that it is not our . . . *your* views which count?' Erika Grossman pouted.

'Of course not, it is the views of the party as expressed through the comrade minister, and that is as it should be, but it is always necessary to have patience.'

'You are quite happy that our links are sound?'

'I'm as satisfied as it is humanly possible to be. The people we are using are staunch and tested members of the party.'

A frown passed across Erika Grossman's brow. In an abstracted voice she said, 'The arrest of the man Crofton in England was singularly unfortunate. I wish we had never known anything about him. As it is, it makes one wonder.'

He smiled at her almost fondly. 'Wasn't it our—yours and my—chosen agents who fed us all that detailed information about the reorganisation of the British Headquarters Signals Group; who compromised that corporal so that he now works for us; who arranged for the car of that nosy journalist to be blown up—with him inside? Those were *our* people, Comrade, who succeeded so splendidly, though each of them required time to achieve results.' His expression became suddenly weary. 'The trouble is, as you and I know, that the needs of our political masters are often out of step with those of our own section. Each has the same dedicated aim, but the methods of approach don't always coincide.' He rose. 'But I beg you to ask the comrade minister to be patient for another week or so and I am certain we shall be able to show him results with which he'll be delighted. Tell him our links with Dahlem are forged in party brotherhood and serve with gratitude the comrade minister and comrade chairman.'

He walked across to the window and gazed out into the yard of the heavily-guarded compound in which the building stood.

'I think,' Comrade Grossman said quietly from her chair, 'that I should like you to accompany me when I go and see the comrade minister tomorrow morning.'

He turned and, clicking his heels, gave her a small bow.

'Naturally,' he said in an expressionless tone.

At about the time this conversation ended, Martin Ainsworth clambered down from the observation platform, agreeably satisfied that he had out-stared the Vopo who had retired from the scene a few minutes earlier.

It was half-past six when he regained the Hotel Lübeck, and though he wasn't certain in what way, he knew he was a different Martin Ainsworth from the one who had set out three hours before. It was as though he had been subjected to one of the livelier fairground amusements and had not only had his liver shaken up, but his mind, too, had somehow become purged.

When he entered the dining-room at seven o'clock, he found that three guests were already at their respective tables. He received their respectful 'Guten Abend' in turn as he moved across to where the rather slatternly girl was pointing.

The grandiloquent descriptions of German dishes had always delighted him, and he was pleased to note that the menu which was now handed him started off with an old friend. 'Tages-Suppe-Doppelkraftbrühe,' it read. From its name he always pictured it as the sort of soup on which Hercules might have trained before undertaking his several labours. In fact—and the present occasion proved to be no exception—it was one of the thinnest and most tasteless fluids he knew. It was followed by 'Butterschnitzel', which was rather good, though it turned out to be nothing more exotic than a flat rissole. The meal finished with cheese and fruit, and he was ready and waiting for Lander well in advance of the appointed hour.

It was hardly the dinner he'd have chosen to sustain him on what was likely to be one of the most exhausting evenings he had ever faced, but perhaps Elli would offer him something.

In his mind's eye he had a sudden vision of her with apfelstrudl in one hand and an automatic pistol in the other. Perhaps he must be ready for either.

6

'I WILL drive you to Wittenbergplatz,' Lander said as Ainsworth got into the car beside him, 'and then you'll be on the direct underground line to Dahlem.'

'Oh!' Ainsworth's tone was scarcely enthusiastic.

'Well, isn't that how you'd normally go?'

'No, I'd take a taxi.'

'To pay a social call on someone you've not seen for twenty-five years: who mayn't be in and from which you may decide to duck out at the last minute?'

'I see what you mean.'

'No, the Martin Ainsworth of this expedition travels by U-Bahn. When he got out at Dahlem Dorf Station, he asks the way to Karolinerstrasse. Incidentally, you must ask someone at the station, so that if any check is made, they will remember and confirm the event. Then, having received his directions, he sets off slowly and thoughtfully, and the nearer he comes to the house, the slower his pace becomes. He crosses over to the other side of the street and gives the house the once-over as he walks past. Then, with apparent decision, he goes up to the door and rings the bell.'

'I would have thought our Martin Ainsworth would have telephoned in advance.'

'He would,' Lander said with a nod. 'But we must sacrifice that natural touch for the element of surprise. It is very important that you arrive on her doorstep without warning. She can't, in the circumstances, refuse to ask you in, but she could easily put you off coming—and would—if you called her in advance.'

Ainsworth wondered what some of his friends in the Temple would think if they could see him now being briefed for an intelligence assignment in a car which for the past few minutes had been going round and round the same square. He could guess what Aunt Virginia's reaction would be.

'And after tonight,' Lander went on, 'we'll have to be very careful about our meetings. It's possible you'll be trailed for a day or two, so it's important that you behave like any other

39

tourist in the city. I'll give you my telephone number and I'd like you to call me there at nine o'clock tomorrow morning. If it's necessary for us to meet, I'll think of something, but I shan't be able to come to the hotel again and you most certainly mustn't be seen anywhere near my office.'

'Where is your office?' Ainsworth asked.

'In Charlottenburg, about a mile from British military headquarters,' Lander replied smoothly.

Ainsworth supposed it probably had a sign outside indicating some harmless activity such as the import of Tunisian dates or darning needles.

'Anything else before I let you out?' Ainsworth shook his head. The moment had arrived for him to be let off the lead. 'Well, good luck.' And then, as though he could read his thoughts, Lander added, 'Nanny won't be far away even if you can't see her.' His mouth twisted into a grin. 'She's a remarkably omniscient nanny.'

The one thing which didn't seem to have changed was the Berlin U-Bahn. There were still the mustard-yellow coaches with a good deal of brass and brown inside. It was about an eight-station ride, and the line ran above ground during the latter part.

About half-a-dozen other people emerged at Dahlem Dorf Station and he let them go ahead of him. He arrived at the top of the staircase and sought directions to Karolinerstrasse from the booking-clerk, whom he engaged in rather more conversation than was strictly necessary in order that the incident might be imprinted on his mind. In fact, a reasonable bump of locality, coupled with his prior study of the street plan, would have enabled him to find his way without assistance.

He stepped on to the pavement outside and turned left. It was exactly half-past eight.

It took him ten minutes, walking along secluded, tree-lined streets, to reach Karolinerstrasse, and he'd ascertained that number fourteen was the last but one house on the right-hand side.

The road curved to the left half-way along, which prevented his obtaining a view of the house until he was two away from it. In any event, even though the houses varied considerably in size and style, each was set back in its own garden and was sheltered from its neighbours by trees and shrubs.

As he approached, he had no difficulty in slowing his pace or in appearing thoughtful. It was years since he had felt so tense and nervous. Not even before a big case in court did the butterflies hatch quite so plentifully in his stomach—as they were now doing.

He crossed the street to obtain a fuller view of the house which he had come up to. It was a small, square, grey stucco building, somewhat newer than its neighbours, and of strictly functional design. It had a flat roof, and, whatever its virtues, none was apparent from the outside. Ainsworth noticed also that a stout, metal fence ran round the outside, and that the front gate appeared to be firmly closed.

He walked on about twenty yards, re-crossed the street and came back to the house. This time, pausing only long enough to give the impression of someone who wishes to make sure he's come to the right address, he seized the handle of the gate and pushed. Even as he did so, he realised that it was locked. It was then that he observed a bell-push let into the pillar, and beneath it what was obviously a combined speaker and microphone.

Holding his breath, he put his finger firmly on the bell-push and waited. At first he thought there was going to be no response and that Lander's intelligence about her always being home on Monday evenings was one of their false turn-ups. Then suddenly a disembodied voice crackled out of the gatepost.

'Wer ist da?'

'Ist das Frau Seidler?' he asked, for the voice, though female, could have been anyone's.

'Ja, aber wer ist da?'

'Ein alter Freund.'

'Und der Name?'

It was obvious that she was not going to recognise his voice any more than he would have hers over this bowdlerising apparatus.

'Martin Ainsworth.' He articulated his name with special care.

There was an immediate gasp from the other end, and almost immediately the front door opened to reveal Elli Seidler, as recognisable as if he had taken leave of her only the week before.

41

'It is Martin,' she exclaimed in English on seeing his head over the top of the gate. She pronounced his name as she had always done, like Martini without its final 'i'. There was a click and the gate swung open and Ainsworth advanced up the short path towards her open arms.

'Oh, Martin,' she gasped, kissing him warmly on both cheeks. 'Mein Gott, what a surprise you have given me! But come in and let me look at you.'

She closed the front door and led him by the hand into the living-room. 'But you are not any older,' she cried out, as she stood back and surveyed him from head to toe. 'The hair is now more distinguished, but the body is still that of a . . . is it sapling?'

'Stripling,' he answered with a grin. 'Though neither is really applicable. But you look wonderful yourself, Elli.'

Though she had put on a considerable amount of weight, and was wearing a somewhat tight, silk dress, which emphasized the bulges brought by the years, her face was almost exactly as it had been twenty-five years before. The skin was smooth and unlined, and the neck was still that of a young girl. But whereas previously she had had very soft, fair hair, it was now a dark chestnut colour.

'Presumably that can't be laid at nature's door,' Ainsworth reflected. His eye went round the room, until it sure enough came to rest on the silver-framed photograph of himself, on a small table in one corner.

'Yes, you see, Martin,' Elli said delightedly, 'you have been here all the time.' She seized his arm and led him to a chair. 'Now sit down, and I shall go and fetch coffee and cake. You still like cake, Martin?'

'I can remember yours as if I've never stopped eating them. Your iced, coffee cake with the nuts was what the heroes used to go to Valhalla for.'

'I have an apfelstrudl made,' she said happily, unaware of the faintly startled frown that flickered across his brow. 'I shall only be a few minutes,' she called out from the door, 'and then, oh what a fine talk we're going to have. So much to tell, so much to ask.'

She disappeared, leaving Ainsworth alone in the room. It was furnished comfortably, though without any ostentation and rather as though she had gone from saleroom to saleroom, buying a chair at this one, a rug at that, and a mirror at another. Nothing matched in the modern sense of reflecting an integrated room: on the other hand none of the pieces actually clashed.

Ainsworth wondered whether she owned the house or rented it, then realised with a jolt that the financial details had probably been attended to by her masters.

Elli a Communist spy! Having seen her again, it did seem incredible, but he would do well not to forget it.

She came back into the room carrying a large tray on which the apfelstrudl sat like a chaste centre-piece.

'Here, Martin,' she said, handing him coffee and a large wedge of the confection, plus a fork to eat it with. 'And now,' she went on, gazing at him as though he were an undreamed-of Christmas present, 'you must tell me all your news, and what you are doing in Berlin again after such a long absence.'

'I'm here on holiday,' he said, in what he hoped reflected an appropriately carefree spirit. 'Berlin is never out of the news and I decided it was high time to see it for myself again.' He grinned at her disarmingly. 'And this summer I've accomplished it.'

'I am so glad. Many people visit Berlin these days. They come to look at the wall'—she pronounced the word as though it was a dirty sound—'and then they go away again. One hopes that they don't forget what they have seen.'

'I'm sure they don't. The whole world is wall conscious. It's a symbol.'

'It's much more than that to us Berliners,' she exclaimed, in a suddenly bitter tone. 'It's something which divides friends and families. It's barbaric, Martin. Does the world realise what it means in terms of misery and suffering?'

'Certainly.'

'I wonder. Where do you live? In London?'

'Yes, in Knightsbridge.'

'Supposing you woke up one morning and found you were cut off from your friends who live in Chelsea or in Hampstead, and it slowly dawned on you that you might never see them again."
She was staring at him intently and he nodded. 'That is how it is here. That is why everyone should come to Berlin and see it and go away and tell what they have seen. In West Berlin we encourage people to look at the wall so that they may realise

what sort of men rule on the other side. We like visitors to photograph the wall and buy picture postcards of it, but if you go into East Berlin you are forbidden to photograph it. There are no picture postcards to buy, and if you take any with you they will be confiscated. And yet they are the ones who built this beautiful wall.' Her voice rang with sarcasm. 'They built it and they are deeply ashamed of it, whatever Mr. Khrushchev may say.' Before Ainsworth could speak, she went on with rising bitterness, 'Do you realise, Martin, that all the gas, electricity and water supplies of the two Berlins are now separate: that if you were in an office in West Berlin and wished to telephone a colleague in East Berlin, whose building you might be able to see from your window, it would take you several hours to make the call and it would have to be routed through Paris or Stockholm, or one of the big international exchanges? And you mightn't get through at all.' She paused slightly breathless. 'I'm sorry, Martin. But life here has certain realities you will not find elsewhere, and though we have learned to adjust ourselves, we would not wish anyone to think that we are reconciled or that we accept the wall and all it symbolises.'

Ainsworth supposed that it was natural in the circumstances that she should not have lost an opportunity of convincing him of her loyalties by condemning those for whom *he* happened to know she worked. She had painted herself in the colours of a hard-boiled, resilient, but highly sensitive, West Berliner. *He* knew them to be false colours.

'I should like to have a look round East Berlin,' he said. 'I understand there are guided tours.'

'For foreigners, yes,' Elli replied. '*You* can visit it if you are prepared to put up with much bureaucratic red tape and to make a donation to Comrade Ulbricht of one West German mark. But it would be easier for *me*'—she pointed a dramatic finger at herself—'to climb the Matterhorn alone and with no greater danger.' She forked a piece of apfelstrudl into her mouth. 'But now, Martin, let us forget Berlin while you tell me about yourself.'

For the next thirty minutes he gave an account of himself, while she listened with animated changes of expression.

'And to think that now you are a famous barrister,' she said when he had finished.

'I never said anything about being famous, Elli.'

44

'But I have seen your name in the English papers, and they only print the most important cases.'

It seemed certain from this that she knew of his participation in the Crofton case.

'My last case certainly achieved the headlines,' he said casually.

'What was that about, Martin?'

'It was one of those spy cases. I defended a man named Crofton who was believed to be working for the Russians.'

'I think, perhaps, I saw about it,' she remarked in a dismissive tone which confirmed Ainsworth's suspicions.

There followed an awkward silence, which he eventually broke by enquiring after some of his fellow students at Pension Seidler.

'Did any of them ever keep in touch with you afterwards, Elli?'

She shook her head. 'The war brought an end to such contacts as I had maintained. But there was only Jean-Pierre and Herzi—you remember her?—and yourself.'

'Were you in Berlin throughout the war?'

'No, I was conscripted and worked in a factory near Hanover. I returned to Berlin in August 1945. Those were terrible days, Martin. We were a conquered nation and our lives and cities lay in ruins. There seemed no prospect of recovery ever. But it is incredible what we have achieved with help.'

'Are you working now?'

'Yes, I run a language school,' she replied, with a smile. 'That is why my English is better now than it was when you first knew me.'

'A language school?' he echoed. 'What languages do you teach and to whom?'

'It is not a big affair, mind you, though it could be larger if I had the space. I don't know if you've heard, Martin, of the new Free University which is situated here in Dahlem. The old university is in East Berlin, of course, but after the war the Ford Foundation provided money for the establishment of a fine new university. There are many foreign students from English-speaking countries and others who cannot speak much German—when they arrive.'

'And that's where your language school comes in?'

'Yes. We run classes not only for them, but also to teach English to German students. You see,' she went on, 'so many text-books, especially technical books, are written in English, and unless the student can read them, he is lost. So we teach English to the Germans and German to all the others,' she added with a laugh.

As she described her work, it occurred to Ainsworth that it could scarcely provide a better front for her more sinister activities.

'I should love to see over your school, Elli,' he said. 'Would that be permitted?'

He was a trifle nonplussed when she agreed to the idea with complete readiness.

Their conversation flitted backwards and forwards in time and reached a point where Ainsworth suddenly said, 'I know what I've been meaning to ask you—what happened to that friend of your husband's, who often used to come to the pension?'

'Which friend do you mean, Martin?' He thought he noted a guardedness in her tone.

'I can't remember his name for the moment. He was tall and rather austere in appearance and his eyes were sunken, but on the occasions that he smiled, his whole face would light up charmingly.'

She shook her head decisively. 'No, I do not know who you mean.'

'You must remember him, Elli. He used to come to supper quite often, and go off to meetings with Wolfgang afterwards.'

'Wolfgang had many friends of that period whom I didn't get to know well.'

Her eyes met Ainsworth's and revealed nothing except that he was hammering on a thrice-locked door. For some reason about which he could only speculate, Elli was not intending to remember her late husband's friend. It was inconceivable that she could have genuinely forgotten him. If only he, Ainsworth, could recall the fellow's name. The quest would now nag him until the name suddenly exploded like a firework in his mind and spelt itself in coloured letters.

The silence which had fallen between them was broken by the telephone ringing. Elli rose and excused herself. She was frowning and looked tense as she left the room. Ainsworth tried without avail to recall having noticed where the telephone was situated.

After she had been gone a minute, he tip-toed across to the

door and quietly opened it. He could hear Elli's muffled voice coming from a back room whose door was also shut. Moving stealthily—he would pretend he was searching for the lavatory if he were discovered—he reached the door and pressed his ear to the keyhole. She was speaking rapidly and in German, but he caught a snatch of the conversation when she said with particular emphasis, 'You know you cannot come to the house. . . . Don't worry, I will arrange something, but you must not come *here*. You understand? On no account must we meet. . . . Now this is what I'll do. Wait a minute while I make sure the door is shut. . . .'

Ainsworth moved like an electric current and was back in the living-room with the door closed behind him before Elli could have had time to lay down the receiver. While he sat waiting for her to rejoin him, his mind dwelt on the fascinating snippet he had overheard. By itself it might not mean very much, but it certainly provided confirmation that she was occupied in serious matters which seemed to have little connection with the activity of running a language school.

'I am so sorry to leave you for such a long time, Martin,' she said with an exaggerated sigh when she came back into the room. 'It was a talkative girl-friend. I thought she would never stop.'

Ainsworth accepted this palpable lie with an agreeable smile. The fact that he now had personal proof of Elli's duplicity somehow made his own two-faced conduct seem less venal. He glanced at his watch.

'I must be going shortly, but first we must make a date for dinner. Will you dine with me tomorrow night, Elli?'

'Tomorrow,' she said dubiously.

'You're the only person I know in Berlin, and if you won't I shall be all alone.'

'How long are you staying?' she asked. 'I don't think you've told me.'

'Perhaps three or four days; perhaps a week. It depends how much I enjoy myself. So dinner tomorrow night?'

'Yes, Martin, that would be nice.' But her response was less than enthusiastic.

'I will come and call for you. At what time?'

'No, it will be easier if I meet you at the restaurant. You tell me where.'

'Where would you like to dine?'

'The Hilton Hotel.'

'You really mean that?'

She nodded. 'It is the one place where one can forget for an hour or two that one is marooned on this tight little island surrounded by the Communist waves. The Hilton is like a luxurious film-set. One hears many different tongues and sees many different faces. Its atmosphere breaks the chains of claustrophobia that we Berliners are often made to feel.' As an afterthought she added, 'And the food is excellent, too.'

'I'll meet you there when? Seven-thirty?'

'Eight o'clock would be better.'

He rose to leave and she made no attempt to detain him. 'How will you go?' she asked as she accompanied him to the door.

'By U-Bahn, the same way as I came.'

'How did you find out where I lived?' she enquired, with a note of interest which Ainsworth failed to understand.

'I looked your address up in the telephone book.' He gave a sheepish grin. 'And in case you're wondering why I didn't call you first, the answer is that I wasn't sure until I arrived outside your front gate whether I was going to have the nerve to ring the bell. If I'd found you living in a four-storey mansion, I'd most likely have retreated. As it is, I'm so glad I didn't. It has been wonderful seeing you again, Elli.' He kissed her on the cheek. 'Good night.'

'Good night, Martin.'

She pressed the button which released the catch on the front gate and watched him until he was out on the pavement. Then giving him a small, almost furtive, wave she quickly closed the door.

As he walked off down the deserted street, Ainsworth had the strongest impression that his departure had been covertly observed. He slid into the dark shadow of a tree and peered back. Sure enough, there was a movement on the far pavement and he was just in time to glimpse a figure as it slithered across a shaft of half-light and merged into tenebrity beyond. Whoever it was, was departing in the opposite direction.

He felt a faint chill of apprehension as he continued on his way. To have your movements secretly watched was a disagreeable sensation, the more particularly when it also induced a sudden feeling of menace. It was with relief that he regained the underground station and further relief when he found himself sitting in the comforting anonymity of a well-filled carriage.

Although Elli had given herself away, he felt reasonably sure that he had not in turn aroused her suspicions. It was only fair to remember, of course, that he had arrived on her doorstep armed with information, of the possession of which she was wholly unaware. How far their first meeting would be thought by Lander to have been fruitful, he didn't know. What he did know was that it had served to clarify his own mind about Elli.

As he thought back over the last two hours, he realised that at some stage a sense of restraint had fallen between them. His mind tried to isolate and pinpoint its cause. Adam and Eve's first rapture had lasted only until they tasted the apple. With him and Elli, perhaps it had been the apfelstrudl which had brought a change in the atmosphere.

7

'A TELEPHONE call for you, Herr Ainsworth,' Fräulein Grimmer announced through the dining-room door. She looked so precisely the same as she had the previous day, even to the slightly lopsided cameo brooch on the upper slope of her bosom, that Ainsworth felt she must have been wrapped in cellophane overnight and left in a medium temperature.

He followed her out of the room and she indicated a telephone on a small table at the top of the stairs.

'Lander here,' a voice announced as he put the receiver to his ear. 'How did things work out last night?'

'Before we go into that, are you satisfied it's safe to talk on this line?' Ainsworth asked, lowering his voice.

'What's bothering you?'

'This telephone.'

'Aren't you in a box?'

'No, I'm on the landing.'

'Well, have it transferred to your bedroom.'

'There isn't an extension there.'

'Oh, really!' Lander sounded exasperated.

'You picked this hotel, I didn't,' Ainsworth retorted unhelpfully.

'You'd better go out to the nearest call-box and ring me from there. But I have an appointment in a quarter of an hour, so please hurry.'

Ten minutes later, when they were speaking again, Ainsworth gave him an account of his evening at Elli's.

'You must try and find out who made the 'phone call,' Lander said.

'How?'

'You must obviously bombard her with your company. When you have dinner with her this evening, you must force the pace. Excuse the simile, but yours must be a whirlwind courtship, not a protracted Victorian romance. You must date her energetically, overcome any hesitations and refuse to take "no" for an answer. You must dominate her with sheer force of personality.'

'You should have brought a dark-eyed hypnotist over, not me,' Ainsworth replied sourly.

'No, no, you can do it. You must succeed. Last night you made a good start, but now we must step up the pace. For example, each time you take her out, you must insist on seeing her home. You must seize every opportunity of getting inside her house.' There was a pause, then Lander said abruptly, 'Incidentally, did you find yourself still physically attracted to her?'

'If you mean,' Ainsworth replied coldly, 'did I want to get into her bed, the answer, last night at any rate, was no.'

'Good. Emotional involvements should be avoided at all costs in our lark. If it is ever necessary to pop into some girl's bed, it should be because the head demands it and not the heart.'

'I'll remember that.'

'Will you call me at this number again tomorrow morning, say between nine and half-past?'

'All right.'

'And you'd better do so from a different box. Did you see anyone follow you when you left the hotel just now?'

'No.'

'Well, keep your eyes open. I shall be surprised if you're not already under observation. Elli will certainly have reported your visit. You know the aphorism about big fleas having little fleas upon their backs to bite 'em, and little fleas having smaller fleas and so *ad infinitum*. It's very much like that with our intelligence brethren in the opposite camp. Till tomorrow.'

When Ainsworth returned to the hotel there was a man polishing a fire hydrant a few yards past the front entrance, another sitting on a delivery tricycle on the other side of the street, apparently doing nothing save breathe in the morning air. Ainsworth glanced at each of them suspiciously, as well as at the approaching postman. He realised that once the insidious seed was sown, it required very little imagination to see sinister designs in the most innocent activity.

He spent no longer back at the hotel than was necessary to collect his camera and travel documents, having decided to go on one of the official tours of East Berlin during the morning which was now at his disposal.

The coaches of Kudos City Tours departed from outside the Zoo station, and it was there that he joined a small throng of like-intended travellers.

'So you want to see East Berlin, eh?' the guide had asked in a gently hectoring tone. She was young and quite pretty apart from being rather hairy. 'O.K., we will let you see the Communist paradise and perhaps you won't want to come back. But somehow I think you will.' They all grinned sheepishly. 'Now will you please give me your passports and also count your money. They will not let you into East Berlin without a currency declaration, and I would warn you that currency offences are amongst the worst you can commit in the paradise on the other side of the wall. Also I must remind you that this tour is for foreigners only. I am not allowed to accompany you. I shall wave goodbye to you at the wall and meet you again on your return—if you return.' Again they grinned dutifully.

At last, with a large honey-bear of a man as driver and with the hairy guide perched beside him, they set off. Immediately a stream of facts and statistics bombarded their ears in English and French as the guide swung into action.

'That building on the right was the headquarters of Adolf Eichmann of whom you have heard.' There followed a few objective biographical details of Eichmann's career and demise.

Ainsworth found himself listening with morbid fascination for the jokes with which she interpolated her commentary. They emerged breathless and with the point often awry, but were delivered with such good will and naïve pleasure that it would have required an ultra-churlish person not to respond with at least a simper.

'And now in a minute I shall be leaving you,' the guide announced, as the coach swung through streets where the devastation had been greatest and where the buildings in use stood in lonely clusters surrounded by open windswept acres. This had once been the heart of Berlin. A second later they turned into Friedrichstrasse and came face to face with the wall at its best-known crossing point.

There was a wooden hut in the middle of the road and Ainsworth could see British, French and American Military Police standing nonchalantly around. Their coach headed past the hut and a young Vopo lifted the striped pole which barred the gap in the wall. A gap which allowed them less than twelve inches free passage on either side. Although the guide had left them, the driver remained to provide a comforting element of stability. Beyond the wall itself further solid barriers jutted out into the road on alternate sides like breakwaters, so that their progress resembled the docking of an unwieldy ship. Eventually, they pulled into a haven and waited.

An armed guard entered the coach and greeted them with a formal salute before moving slowly down the aisle and examining their passports. There was a further wait after he had departed, and Ainsworth gazed out at the scene. They were only twenty yards inside the wall, and through one of the gaps he could still see the nonchalantly lounging military police. There was a group of camera-pointing tourists on the observation platform which lay within a few yards of the wall on the west side. From time to time the striped pole was raised to let a car pass, and there was a queue of people waiting to pass through the East German control hut. Fifty yards up the road he could see a small throng of bystanders looking towards the checkpoint, and realised that this was as close as they could approach on their side.

The driver, who had been chatting to a woman and two men outside the coach, now rejoined it, accompanied by one of the men, who looked like a small, plump, bespectacled seal.

'Welcome to democratic Berlin,' the seal announced, in curiously pinched English. He blinked at them as though uncertain of his reception, which Ainsworth reflected he might have good reason to be.

A few minutes later they had manoeuvred past the last obstacle.

'In this part of Berlin,' said the seal, 'you see much damage caused in the war against Fascism.' He waved his hand at a green mound on which a couple of rabbits were hopping in leisurely fashion. 'That is the site of the Hitler bunker.'

With a shock, Ainsworth realised that they were in the Wilhelmstrasse, the pre-war seat of government, and that there was now only untidy open space where previously ministries had stood. At the top of the street, the Adlon Hotel, which had once been Berlin's pride, loomed like a salvaged wreck. A few seconds later he was looking at the Brandenburg Gate from the other side, beyond it the sweep of wall over which he had peered the previous afternoon. He found it an uncanny experience, and all the while the seal bubbled on with information about the war against Fascism and its victims.

Unter den Linden reflected but a shadow of its former glory, its only building of any solidity being the new Soviet Embassy. At the far end the great public buildings of old squatted, each in its setting of isolated desolation. The cathedral appeared to be a decaying shell, its dome resembling a rusty dish cover.

But, the seal assured them, there were plans to restore each and every one of the crumbling edifices and completion dates tripped off his tongue like odds off a bookmaker's.

'And here you see the fine new Marx-Engels Square where we hold our parades.'

Ainsworth gazed out in awe at a space which made the Horse Guards Parade seem a cabbage patch by comparison. Along one side was a vast tiered stand with a prominent saluting platform in its centre.

Now they began to move away from the ruined centre of the city and into more populated streets as they penetrated eastwards. People paused and watched them pass with impassive expressions, though occasionally a child would smile and wave, and once a group of teddy-boys laughed derisively.

'Here is a state bakery,' said the seal enthusiastically, and went on to tell them how many loaves of bread it baked each day.

'Here is a famous park . . . here a new cinema for the people . . . here apartments for the workers.'

Obediently Ainsworth and his fellow-passengers looked out this side and that. So this was Herr Ulbricht's Berlin, this was the paradise towards which Elli was bending all her efforts. Ainsworth's main impression was of dowdiness. No one looked hungry, far less famished, and everyone appeared amply clothed, but there was a uniform drabness wherever the eye roamed. The buses, the trams and the motor cars were the same as their counterparts in the western sectors of the city, but in greater need of a touch of paint. Indeed, it seemed to Ainsworth that the only splashes of colour were provided by the banners which festooned many of the buildings and which proclaimed Herr Ulbricht to be the people's champion.

'And now we shall leave the bus and visit the great Soviet War Memorial in Treptower Park,' announced the seal with the air of one who enjoys providing treats.

They followed him out, pleased to stretch their legs along a broad, tree-lined walk.

'Every piece of plant you see came from the Soviet Union.

And here we have the figure of a Russian mother grieving for her lost sons.'

Ainsworth found himself gazing at one of those larger than life Russian statutes and receiving the same impression as from a photograph which has been blown up beyond artistic expediency.

On they trooped up a broad, paved slope towards two vast stone buttresses which bestrode the summit. All the while the seal poured out information. How many Soviet soldiers had been killed in the fighting to free Berlin from the Fascists, how many were buried in the area which was about to come under their gaze. And as Ainsworth listened, he tried to recall what other nation had so assiduously built war memorials on the soil of those they had conquered. Or freed, as the seal insistently put it.

Suddenly he was looking from the top of the slope at a superbly symmetrical green hillock about a quarter of a mile away, from which rose up a gigantic statue of a Soviet soldier with a broken Swastika under his feet. Between where they stood and the monument lay smaller memorials on either side, and beneath which thousands more dead were buried. The green hillock itself was the tomb of several thousand, the seal explained.

It was indeed an impressive scene, the more so because of the superb care with which it was tended. There was not a blade of grass out of order, and the seal was obviously well satisfied by the impact of his conducted pilgrimage.

'We will now return to the bus,' he said, when he considered they had drunk their fill.

They reached the road to find that the bus was now in a large car park fifty yards away on the other side. At the entrance to the car park stood a kiosk with a number of fly-blown postcards hanging round it like Tibetan banners. Ainsworth, however made his way across to a barrow where he had noticed their driver talking to the old man in charge of it.

At one end were some bottles of a syrupy-looking drink, at the other some postcards showing views of the war memorial and of one of the huge parades in Marx-Engels Square. He selected a couple of cards, but the old man shook his head crossly when he tendered West German money and snatched them back. Ainsworth shrugged and turned away. He felt slightly nettled until he realised that the old man had most probably reacted out of fear. For an East German to be found in possession of West German marks was a grave crime, indeed. His last view as the coach pulled away was of the old man dusting his wares with the pathetic remains of a feather brush. It seemed likely that his stock collected dust a good deal quicker than he could sell it.

The highlight of the return journey was the drive along the Karl-Marx Allee.

'It used to be called the Stalin Allee,' the seal explained.

'What d'you change the name for?' an American asked, but the seal ignored the interruption.

It was a broad, impressive boulevard lined with apartment houses, from a number of which the tiled veneer was peeling, shops and restaurants. As they approached its western end, the seal pointed out yet newer buildings of exotic architecture.

'See how well the people look,' he crowed. 'In democratic Berlin there are no slums. Everyone has a nice home. There are fine schools and hospitals. . . .'

'And prisons and cemeteries,' a voice behind Ainsworth muttered.

'The children are happy because they know they will be able to go to the university.'

'This guy makes me want to throw up,' the voice behind Ainsworth said impatiently.

'Ssh, Harry, he'll hear you.'

'Let him, the little pink punk.'

A few minutes later they were steering their way back through the barren wasteland of central Berlin towards the international checkpoint.

The same guard came on board to examine each passport solemnly once more as if he expected to unmask some hideous plot of swapped identities.

Then the seal bade them farewell from democratic Berlin and thanked them for coming, and the coach moved slowly, slowly back through the wall. As the pole was lowered behind them, everyone let out a silent sigh of relief and glanced expectantly at his neighbour.

'So you have come safely back from the workers' paradise!' Their West Berlin guide cast an ironical eye over them. 'You have been where I'm not allowed to go! I am not permitted to visit my grandmother or my cousins. Already since 1960 I have not seen them. Once I send my grandmother a big food parcel, but the Communists keep it until everything is bad and then they deliver it.'

If she meant to make them feel uncomfortable, she succeeded, though Ainsworth found himself resentful of the fact. But then it is never agreeable having one's conscience used for a pin cushion.

As the bus drew away, the guide announced, 'And now we go and visit the Bernauerstrasse where the wall is one side of the street and you can see where many have lost their lives trying to escape from paradise. Here in Berlin brother shoots brother,' she added with a grim little smile.

Ainsworth was not prepared for the sight which met his eyes in Bernauerstrasse. He had read something about it, but seeing it could be described only as a mind-searing experience. One side of the street was normal with shops and apartments, the other was dead. Every doorway, every window along its entire length was bricked up and coils of barbed wire ran over the roof-tops. A church which stood a few yards back from the pavement appeared intact . . . behind a twelve-foot wall. Once the butcher and the grocer had faced each other across the street in neighbourly competition. The grocer still traded, but all that was left of the butcher was the flaking sign above his blocked-out door.

At a road intersection a number of Vopos were standing on a platform in the killing ground their side of the wall. They were laughing and joking, and the oldest didn't look more than twenty-two or twenty-three. They were good-looking boys, and Ainsworth had to force himself to realise that they wouldn't hesitate to use their weapons to kill—if necessary, each other. Just in front of them against his side of the wall was propped a wreath and above it an improvised plaque. Here on the 28th September, 1961, Gunther Reitke, aged 20, had been shot and killed whilst trying to escape.

Ainsworth turned away feeling sick. Here surely man's long history of inhumanity to man had attained a level of such evil refinement as would be unsurpassed should life continue even a million years.

He was glad he had seen all he had this day. His lawyer's training might have cautioned him that there were always two sides to every question, but nothing, *nothing*, could excuse the brutal obscenity of the wall. It had been built by those whom

57

Elli served, and gone now were his last qualms about deceiving her.

'I shan't be in to dinner tonight,' he told Fräulein Grimmer, when he arrived back at the hotel. She was sitting at the receipt of custom with a large ledger open before her.

'It is included,' she said primly.

'That's all right.'

'I cannot make any reduction, you see everything is ordered.'

'I quite understand.' Anyway it was the British taxpayer's bill and he had no intention of entering into an argument to save the treasury a German mark or two.

'Have there been any messages for me while I've been out?' he asked.

'None, Herr Ainsworth.'

He had half-expected to find one from Elli calling off their dinner engagement, and had been wondering what he should do in this event.

He was thankful it hadn't arisen, and decided to go and lie on his bed for half an hour and lay his plans for the evening. Almost immediately, however, he dropped off to sleep, though not before letting out a cry of remembrance as the name of Wolfgang Seidler's friend landed like a meteor in his mind. Part of his name, anyway. It was Gustav.

8

THE lobby of the hotel certainly bore out what Elli had said, and presented as cosmopolitan a scene as anyone could wish. Telephone bells rang incessantly, lifts disgorged men in cool, freshly pressed silk suits and women in fashions straight from Paris and Rome. Small bell-hops in uniform left the head-porter's desk in relays, to return, like boomerangs, a few minutes later, their commissions fulfilled.

Ainsworth had just completed a reconnaissance of the ground-floor region and returned to the lobby when he saw Elli paying off her taxi. She was wearing a sleeveless dress of royal blue and carrying a fur cape over one arm. Her hair had also clearly received professional attention. He advanced towards the door.

'Elli!' He clasped her hands in his and kissed her. 'You look absolutely stunning.'

She beamed with pleasure. 'I am all right to be escorted by a famous English lawyer?'

'The Lord Chief Justice himself would be jealous if he could see me.' He slipped his arm through hers and piloted her across the lobby. 'Tonight we'll really celebrate. I've already warned the barman to stand by for champagne cocktails. Nothing less will do, even though you mayn't like them.'

'But I do, Martin,' she said, giving his arm a small squeeze. 'I adore champagne cocktails.'

The waiter led them to a table in a corner of the bar and brought the drinks.

'To Elli,' Ainsworth whispered conspiratorially, raising his glass and smiling at her over the top. 'To Elli of yesterday, Elli of today and Elli of tomorrow.'

'Thank you, Martin, you are very sweet,' she replied, though he thought he detected a slightly troubled note in her voice.

Overcoming her hesitation he ordered a second round of champagne cocktails and asked for the menu to be brought.

'Why don't you come to England for a holiday, Elli?' he urged in a suddenly serious voice. 'A proper holiday, I mean, stay six weeks or a couple of months. We have a very comfortable spare bedroom and Aunt Virginia would love to meet you.' He was pleasurably startled by the sincerity of his performance and could just picture Aunt Virginia's outraged expression if she'd been present as a fly on the wall. 'It would do you good,' he went on, 'and anyone can see that you need a rest. Why don't you, Elli? I should love having you and showing you around.' He hoped his words gave additional promise of all manner of unmentioned possibilities.

For several seconds she seemed to hover over her reply, then she said, 'I am tempted, Martin, but'—and she shook her head sadly—'it is impossible, I cannot leave my work.'

'Why not? Nobody's indispensable and I'm quite sure the language school would manage without you for a few weeks.'

'It is too difficult.'

'There's no difficulty in it. It's because you're run down and in need of a decent break that you see difficulties. A holiday in England is just what you need to restore your sense of perspective.'

'Why are you suddenly asking me like this, Martin?' She watched him gravely.

'I've been thinking about it ever since I left your house yesterday evening, and this afternoon I made up my mind. Please come, Elli.'

She shook her head miserably. 'I can't. I can't.'

'But why not? Are you frightened of something?'

'Of course not. I've told you, I can't leave my work.'

His brow furrowed in thought. 'Supposing I make all the arrangements: supposing I even fix up for someone to look after the school while you're away.'

'How could you? You know nothing about it, Martin. You don't know what's involved.'

'There's something else, too, isn't there?' he asked quietly.

'What do you mean?'

'You're worried about something, I can tell. What is it, Elli? Have you forgotten how I was able to help you once before?'

'How could I ever forget that!'

Her eyes glistened with tears, though he was unsure whether they were caused by recollection of the past, or were the effect of his emotional onslaught.

Biting his lip and in a voice which he had no difficulty in making sound embarrassed, he said, 'It would bring me great happiness to help you again, Elli.'

She dabbed her eyes with her handkerchief. 'Please don't go on, Martin. Perhaps it was a mistake to meet again after such a long time. Each of us has altered: we are not the same Martin and Elli of twenty-five years ago. We cannot recapture those days: too much has happened.'

'Nonsense,' he replied robustly. 'And anyway I'm not trying to recapture the past, I just want to live the present. Fundamentally, we're the same two people as we were then, and with the same ideals and hopes. You happen to be living in what might be called the western world's look-out post. More than most of us, you can see with your own eyes the realities of Communist government. It's the difference between having a street accident happen outside your own window and in the next town. Living here must become appallingly oppressive, and I can understand why Berliners are so sensitive about the status of their city.' He drained his glass. 'On the other hand, a two-hour tour of East Berlin this morning has proved to me—not that I really required proof—that on the political front there are no blacks or whites, just various shades of grey.' He observed her closely as he spoke. 'Herr Ulbricht's Berlin is not all that different from Herr Brandt's. The difference, perhaps, between Bond Street and Lambeth Walk. And there are a whole lot of people who prefer Lambeth Walk, anyway.'

He paused and gave a small Gallic shrug. He would dearly have liked to be able to see into Elli's head and assess the effect of his words. He had gone as far as he thought discreet in declaring sentiments of a politically ambivalent nature. He obviously couldn't pretend at this delicate juncture to be a full-blooded secret supporter of the Communist cause. He now awaited Elli's reaction, uncomfortably aware that she had him under intense scrutiny.

Abruptly she turned away and picked up the menu. 'Shall we order, Martin?' she said.

Without showing the slight sense of chagrin he experienced, he reached for the menu and embarked with apparent gusto on a discussion of its items.

Their table was candle-lit and set against one wall of the restaurant, which was about three-quarters full. The atmosphere was as protective and soothing as a fur-lined bean pod, but Ainsworth decided to recommence his war of nerves, though on a different front.

'By the way, Elli, I've remembered the name of that friend of Wolfgang's I was trying to recall last night.' There could be no mistaking the fact, she suddenly stiffened. 'Yes, it was Gustav.'

'Gustav?' she repeated nervously. 'What was his other name?'

'That still escapes me, but surely you remember Gustav. He was always round at the pension. Tallish chap with deep set eyes, a very attractive slow smile, and rather a funny walk. His surname was von something or other.'

'I think his name is vaguely familiar, but you clearly remember more about him than I do, Martin.'

'He had pronounced left-wing views,' Ainsworth added casually.

Elli shook her head. 'So many people used to come in those days, and I saw none of them again after Wolfgang's death.'

'I'd have felt sure you'd have remembered Gustav.'

'Gustav, Werner, Karl, I cannot now remember which was which.' She picked up her wine glass and took a sip. 'This is a very nice wine, Martin,' she said. 'And was I not right in saying that it was a very good restaurant?'

'Right as always, Elli.'

He forebore to point out that as yet they'd tasted no food and that her switch of conversation had been as elegant as a rhinoceros charge. He now knew for certain that Elli and her husband's friend were still in touch with each other. Last night she had denied his existence: tonight, confronted by part of his name, she had changed her ground. On both occasions she had reacted nervously. There could be only one explanation, and when Ainsworth recalled Gustav's previous political leanings and Elli's current allegiance, one did not have to speculate very far. At all costs, he must remember the man's surname. If necessary he would comb the telephone directory from first page to last. Once he saw the name, he was confident that he would recognise it.

Meanwhile, their food had arrived and he wouldn't spoil it by the introduction of further inhibiting subjects. It was indeed an excellent meal, and as they ate they discussed nothing more dangerous than music and theatre and books, in which they shared a lively and well-informed interest.

It was while they were on the qualities of Brecht that Ainsworth became aware of a young man approaching their table. He wore an unpleasantly knowing smile, and it was soon apparent that they were the object of his attention.

'I think there's somebody coming over who knows you,' he he said in an aside to Elli, who hadn't noticed the young man's approach.

Elli looked up sharply—too sharply for someone who wasn't permanently alerted to danger—and he observed a fleeting expression of annoyance and suspicion, before it was replaced by one of polite acceptance of what was an unavoidable situation.

'Good evening, Frau Seidler,' the young man said, with an ingratiating smile. His look fell boldly on Ainsworth.

'Martin, this is Herr Koeslin, who is a student at my school,' Elli said. 'Mr. Ainsworth.'

Koeslin brought his heels together and gave Ainsworth a Germanic head bow as they shook hands across the table. He must have been in his late twenties, had hair which, but for the fact it was cut en brosse, would have sprouted in several different directions, and lacked colour in his cheeks, which were pasty except at the sides of his chin which looked sore from shaving. His eyes were grey and matched his bow tie.

The conversation had so far been in German, but he now said in uncomfortably articulated English, 'You are from England, Mr. Ainsworth?'

'Yes,' Ainsworth said in an agreeable tone.

'And this is your first time in Berlin?'

'The first time for a long time, shall we say.'

'But I have noted that you can understand German.'

'Not as well, I'm sure, as you do English.'

Koeslin jerked his head in another little bow. 'All I know of English, I owe to Frau Seidler—she is a very good teacher.' When Elli made no acknowledgment of the compliment, he went on, 'How long do you stay in our city, Mr. Ainsworth?'

'Only a few days and then I'm flying down to the Bavarian Alps.' Well he might at that, but he saw no reason to be overmeticulous in satisfying Herr Koeslin's curiosity.

'The mountains are so much healthier than Berlin,' Koeslin replied with a bland smile. It might have been a warning of some sort: on the other hand it might have been nothing more than Herr Koeslin's odd English. Ainsworth wondered, but until the young man had left them he couldn't do more than this.

'I must go home to my studies,' he said, straightening up in readiness for further heel-clicking and head jerking, 'or Frau Seidler will be cross with me in the morning.' He lifted Elli's hand to his lips and shook Ainsworth's vigorously, then strode out of the restaurant.

'I do not like that young man,' Elli said before Ainsworth had time to start asking any questions.

'What's wrong with him?' he enquired in an innocent tone.

'I just don't like him.'

'How long has he been one of your students?'

She shrugged. 'A month, perhaps.'

'What's his background?'

She gave another shrug, this time indicating impatience as well as indifference. 'I believe he wishes to study nuclear physics at the university, but I am not sure.'

'He seemed quite an eager and intelligent young man.'

'It would seem that he was here alone,' she said slowly, as if speaking her thoughts aloud.

'We'll soon find out. Waiter!' The head waiter in charge of their section of the restaurant came up. 'Did you notice a young man talking to us just now?'

'Jawohl, mein Herr.'

'He came from somewhere the other side. I'd like to know whether he was dining alone or with somebody.'

'I find out.' They saw him go across and speak to a group of waiters on the far side of the room. 'He was here alone,' he said on his return. 'He had a light dinner of soup and salad.'

'Thank you very much.'

'Bitte sehr, mein Herr.'

'Well that answers that,' he said affably to Elli, but it was apparent that the encounter had bothered her for some unexplained reason. She seemed impatient to leave, but Ainsworth affected not to notice, lingered over his coffee and ordered a liqueur as an after-thought.

Eventually, she was driven to say, 'Martin, I'm terribly sorry but I have a headache. I wonder if——'

'I'll get the bill right away,' he broke in solicitously, pleased as a schoolboy that he had forced her into the open. 'Was it the champagne, do you think?'

'No, no. I felt it coming on before I arrived. I usually have something in my bag to take, but tonight not. I am so sorry, Martin, to spoil our evening.'

'We'll be able to have lots more, so don't worry.' He steered her towards the door. 'I'll take you home in a taxi.'

'Please, Martin, no,' she said with surprising urgency. 'I shall be all right and it is such a long ride to Dahlem, and your hotel is so near.'

'You really have forgotten me, Elli,' he said smoothly, 'if you think I would let a girl-friend who isn't feeling well find her own way home.'

He linked his arm firmly through hers as they passed into the lobby.

She was silent for the greater part of the journey, casting him an occasional wan smile as she dabbed at her forehead with a cologne-scented handkerchief. Shortly before they reached their destination, she slipped her hand into his and said, 'I hope you will excuse me if I do not ask you in, Martin, but I think I will go straight to bed.'

'Just what I was going to suggest, anyway,' he replied with an approving nod. 'Once you're safe and sound inside your own house, I shall leave you.'

'Then you'll keep the taxi.'

'No, I think I'll let it go. I'll return by U-Bahn. I'll enjoy the walk either end.'

'Why not keep the taxi?' Her tone was agitated. 'It will be much better for you.'

'I can always find another, if necessary.'

'That is the point, they are very difficult to find near me at this hour of the evening. Really, Martin, you should go home in this one, you won't be able to find another.'

'I probably 'shan't want to, and anyway, I'll risk it.'

The driver, after directions from Elli, turned into Karoliner-strasse and pulled up in front of her darkened house. Ainsworth paid the fare, added a fat tip and helped Elli out.

'Give me your key and I'll open the gate,' he said, holding out his hand.

'I will do it,' she muttered in an embarrassed tone. 'It is some-times difficult. . . .'

She managed to obscure her action from his view, but it was apparent from the amount of manipulation which went on that this was no ordinary lock, nor yet one which was, as she put it, difficult.

As the gate swung open, she turned to him with a strained smile. 'I am sorry to have spoilt the evening with my silly headache. And now you have a long journey home.'

'Not quite yet, Elli. I'm not leaving until I see you safely inside the house.'

She bit her lip, then with a small, exasperated sigh, she walked the few yards to the front door. Again she was at pains to prevent his seeing how she opened it. All he knew was that she might have been opening an intricate safe from the amount of time it took her.

She stepped inside, switched on a light, and stood suddenly stock still.

'What's the matter?' he asked, experiencing a frisson of apprehension himself.

It seemed an age before she moved or spoke.

'Matter? Nothing.' She now turned and in effect barred his entry.

'Elli, tell me what's wrong?' he said in a tone of pleading. 'You can't fool me, I know you too well. Something's worrying you, you're on edge. It's as though you're still living under the secret police and are scared of every footfall.' He made a move as if to thrust past her.

'You can't come in, Martin . . . my headache. . . .'

'What was it that frightened you when you opened the front door just now? And don't tell me nothing, I saw the way you suddenly stiffened.'

'It was . . . I thought I heard a sound but I must have been mistaken. My head . . .'

'In that event, I'm not leaving until I've had a look into every room.'

'Please, Martin! It was as you say my nerves.'

'If there's a burglar hanging about, we'll soon find out,' he said in what he hoped was a loud enough tone to scare off anyone who might indeed be lurking in the house. Though he'd heard nothing to arouse his own suspicions, Elli equally clearly had. Or if not heard, then seen, or noticed something.

He felt anything but brave, but things were moving his way and he couldn't afford not to exploit this moment of opportunity.

Pushing past her, he opened the living-room door and switched on the light. It appeared perfectly normal.

'You'd better have a look too, Elli, just to make sure nothing's been tampered with.'

She peered past him. 'No, it is all right. I was mistaken, there is nothing wrong.'

'You can say that when we've been over the rest of the house and found everything all right,' he declared firmly.

As he turned back into the hall, he glanced at her and was startled by what he saw. She looked like a creature trapped on the top floor of a burning house, and he had to remind himself sharply of Bernauerstrasse and the grim wall winding through the city like a poisonous snake, not to take her in his arms and give her comfort and reassurance. But this was the cold war reduced to a personal level and he mustn't throw away his advantage.

He went next into the kitchen. The windows were closed and he could see nothing wrong. The only other downstairs room turned out to be a small study. He noticed the telephone on a large roll-top desk which was firmly closed. Did people normally shut their desks when not in actual use? He thought not, as he gazed at its corrugated, sliding top.

Elli walked over and tried the top. It held fast and she let out an audible sigh of relief.

'I keep my money in there,' she said. 'There can't have been a burglar or he would have broken it open.'

'Good! But let's just have a look upstairs.'

There were two bedrooms, one of which was small and only partly furnished, and a combined bathroom and lavatory. There wasn't a sign of disturbance in any of them.

As they returned downstairs, Ainsworth felt his advantage was slipping away from him, an impression which was enhanced by Elli's own improved spirits.

'Thank you, Martin,' she said, moving resolutely towards the front door. 'Once more you have been the gallant Englishman in my life.' There was a note of irony in her voice.

He must make one final effort to break through her defences. Seizing her in his arms, he kissed her warmly on the lips, then buried his face in the softness of her neck.

'Oh, Elli, my darling, I'm so worried about you. If you'd only tell me what's wrong, I could help you. What is it, darling?'

He felt her relax in his embrace. 'Why don't you come to England with me? Leave behind here whatever it is that's troubling you. Forget Berlin and all its tensions.' He brushed his hand gently across her brow. 'Say, yes, you will, and I'll have everything arranged before you get up tomorrow morning.'

'Oh, Martin,' she whispered through a long sigh which he felt ripple through her entire body. 'One day, perhaps, I will tell you, but now I cannot.'

'What is it, Elli?' he urged. 'Don't you trust me?'

'Of course I trust you, but it is something I cannot talk about and I cannot come to England yet. Later, perhaps, if you still want me.'

He felt a slight chill of uneasiness. *If you still want me.* The self-satisfied Bowes had got him into this: if necessary he would have to extricate him, and that covered the emotional entanglement, too.

'Is it . . . that you're tied up with some . . . organisation?'

'I can't talk about it, Martin. Please don't ask me any more questions.'

'So you are!' he said, holding his head back and gazing straight into her face. 'I thought I was right.'

She attempted to disengage herself from his arms, but he held her. 'You must go, Martin.'

'Elli,' he began, fixing her attention on his own face; 'who are you working for? The Americans? The British?'

'Martin, you mustn't ask me these questions,' she cried out in anguish.

'Not the Russians? Surely not the Russians?' He went on urgently, 'Wolfgang, was he a Communist? Is that why he was arrested? Elli, Elli, you *must* tell me the truth.'

Well, there it was, the frontal assault. If she withstood it, he would have to withdraw and regroup his forces.

'You know me better than anyone, Martin,' she said lightly touching his cheek with her hand. 'I promise you that I am doing nothing of which I need to be ashamed. And now you must leave, Martin. My head is really very bad.'

Hoist by my own ruddy petard, he reflected ruefully, and with an answer which would have done credit to the Delphic oracle herself.

'I'll call you tomorrow morning,' he managed to say.

'I shall be at the school all day.'

'Will you come out with me again tomorrow evening, Elli?'
Forlornly he added, 'I don't know how much longer I shall be
staying.'

Somewhat to his surprise, she readily agreed, but insisted that
they should eat at a small restaurant not far from where she
lived.

'The Hilton is for celebrations. Tomorrow we are old friends
dining simply.'

She stood at the front door and watched him walk towards
the gate, which sprang open with a little buzz as he reached it.
She had disappeared inside the house, however, by the time
he'd closed it and turned to wave.

He paused a few yards along the pavement and slipped into
the shadows. At length, satisfied that no one had been observing his departure on this occasion, he set off for the U-Bahn
station at a brisk pace. As the train made its leisurely progress
towards the centre of the city, he cast his mind over the evening's event in an endeavour to draw up a sort of profit-and-loss
account.

On the profit side, Elli had as good as admitted being engaged
in intelligence activities. Since this was a fact already known to
him, however, the only element of profit lay in the condition
of mind he had induced in her to make the admission. On the
loss side, he had used up almost all his resources and still not
sufficiently gained her confidence. The fact that he was now
more certain than ever of her complicity as a Communist spy
made failure a sourer prospect than he had previously contemplated.

He must try to find out more about Koeslin, whose sudden
appearance at their table had so obviously disconcerted Elli.
Perhaps Lander could help over that.

More than anything, however, he wished he knew what it
was that had alarmed her as she'd opened the front door. She
had scented sudden danger, of that he was sure. But in what
shape or form remained a puzzle to nag his mind for the rest
of the journey and long afterwards.

While Ainsworth was rumbling home beneath the streets of
West Berlin, Hans Fröhlich was pacing up and down the duty
room in the government building in which he worked in East
Berlin. In one corner stood a small transmitting and receiving
set which at the moment was emitting an expectant hum but

69

nothing more. From time to time he cast it an impatient glance and consulted his watch, while from the walls Comrades Lenin and Ulbricht looked down in eternal watchfulness.

He was due to be relieved by a colleague in half an hour, and was particularly anxious that the message he awaited should come through before then. The Dahlem operation was his direct responsibility, and the fact that it was in a ticklish phase made his presence in the duty room more than ever desirable when contact with their link was made.

It was twenty-three minutes to eleven which meant that contact was already seven minutes overdue. And seven minutes in his twilight field spelt four-hundred-and-twenty possibilities of things gone wrong. One for every second.

The set let out a sudden low whine, and the red light which had been shining with basilisk intensity abruptly vanished. At the same time a metallic voice filled the room.

'Seagull reporting to control.' Fröhlich threw a switch. 'Go ahead, Seagull.'

'Meeting most urgent. Will control arrange.'

'Will arrange. Tomorrow. Time and place as known to Seagull.'

A click indicated that the call was finished. Fröhlich switched off the set and went and stared out of the window. He stood perfectly still while thoughts raced through his mind.

For Seagull to ask for a meeting could mean only one thing. A climax was at hand. In the light of instructions which were explicit on the subject, no other interpretation was possible. Moreover, there had been a note of suppressed tension in that disembodied voice which had underlined the dramatic tenseness of the message. For an agent as experienced as Seagull to sound such a note of urgency was disturbing.

Fröhlich turned back into the room and met Lenin's frown with one of his own. Well, he had been right about one thing. The comrade minister was not going to have to wait very long before events began turning in Dahlem.

In the middle of the night Ainsworth woke up, and with a sudden spasm of recollection shot bolt upright in bed and exclaimed to his empty room, 'Von Sternmeier. That was his name. Gustav von Sternmeier.'

9

IMMEDIATELY after breakfast the next morning, he wrote a post-card to Aunt Virginia. It bore the wish-you-were-here-having-a-lovely-time theme, and was as innocuous as if it had been true. In fact, the thought of Aunt Virginia in Berlin was enough to make him roll his eyes heavenwards. That done, he went out to the call-box to telephone Lander.

The day showed every sign of repeating yesterday's pattern. After he had made his progress report, he would have the morning and afternoon to himself and would spend the evening once more with Elli. But how much longer would it continue this way?

'Where are you speaking from?' Lander asked as soon as the call was through.

'The same place as yesterday.'

'Were you followed?'

As a matter of fact, this possibility had slipped Ainsworth's mind. 'I don't think so,' he replied uncertainly.

'Well, make sure you're not when you leave.'

'I'll do my best.'

'It's very important,' Lander said a trifle testily.

Ainsworth decided to ignore his tone. This was security-mindedness at its stuffiest and most irritating. Lander was behaving like a bunch of school prefects waiting to catch Smith minor smoking in the lav.

'Do you want me to tell you what happened last night?'

'Very much, but not over the telephone. We must meet this morning. Can you manage in half an hour's time?'

'Yes, but where?'

'I'm about to tell you. Go to the Zoo U-Bahn Station and on to the platform for a train to Leopoldplatz. There's a clock on the platform. Get into the first train which arrives after half-past ten. Is that clear?'

'Yes.' Ainsworth tried to make his tone sound bored to offset Lander's note of accepted superiority.

'If a train comes in at twenty-nine minutes past ten, what will you do?'

'Give it a sugar bun.'

'Mr. Ainsworth, this is not a jesting matter.'

'Nor am I a backward child. If I'm to board the first train after half-past ten, then I obviously don't get into one which arrives at twenty-nine minutes past. Am I right?'

'Yes.'

'Well, credit me in future with having a bit more *nous.*'

'I'm sorry,' Lander said stiffly. 'I just wanted to make quite sure you understood.'

'And now you have, so go on.'

'Get into the third carriage from the front. I'll join you in it.'

'O.K.'

'Any questions?'

'Absolutely none.'

Ainsworth strode back to the hotel still smarting under Lander's donnish arrogance. Well, he'd do as he had been instructed, and he didn't care one way or another whether the plan worked, except that he would derive a certain amount of grim satisfaction if Lander failed to appear.

When he left the hotel ten minutes later to walk to the underground station, he did, however, glance about him to see if he was being followed and, indeed, take evasive action to throw any unseen pursuer off his trail. But so far as he was able to tell, no one was showing the smallest interest in him. At the Zoo Station, where a number of lines converged, he did some further dodging about, and arrived on the platform with three minutes to spare. Within a few seconds a train came in and absorbed all the waiting passengers apart from himself. He looked quickly up and down the platform and was satisfied that he hadn't been followed. Fresh people began to arrive and he moved to where he estimated the third coach would pull up.

A distant rumble indicated the approach of a train and he glanced up at the clock. Its hands showed one minute after the half-hour. He looked about him anxiously, but there was still no sign of Lander.

'Does this train go to Leopoldplatz?' he asked an official as it came bounding out of the tunnel.

'Jawohl.'

One, two, three, he counted, this was the right coach. The doors snapped to behind him and with a jerk the train set off again. At the same moment a smooth voice beside him said, 'Good morning, Mr. Ainsworth.'

Ainsworth turned his head to find Lander standing next to him. 'Hello. I didn't see you on the platform.'

'I got on at the station before. It seemed wiser.'

'Oh! I don't think I was followed.'

'I don't think you were, otherwise we shouldn't be talking in this way. I'd have kept away. But you must learn to relax.'

'I'm perfectly relaxed,' Ainsworth replied loftily.

'You weren't as the train came in. I could see you.' A smile flickered across his face. 'Now don't get cross again. After all, I expect you tell people how to behave in the witness box before they go into court, so why should you become upset when I give you a hint or two about the cloak-and-dagger trade?'

'As they say in American film court scenes, the point is well taken,' Ainsworth replied with a grin.

'Good.' Lander looked up and down the coach. 'We might as well sit down. There are two seats at the end.' When they were seated, he went on, 'Now tell me about last night.'

When Ainsworth had finished his recital of events, Lander pursed his lips and said in a restrained tone, 'Perhaps you'll get further this evening. We must hope so.'

Ainsworth felt dashed. It wasn't that he was expecting paeans of praise, but he had thought there was enough on the credit side to ensure a satisfied listener. Lander had shown the barest interest in the description of Koeslin's intervention and dismissed its significance with a shrug.

Lander now went on, emphasising his meaning by gently thumping his knee with a fist. 'We mustn't lose sight of our objective which is to find out Frau Seidler's method of communication with her East Berlin masters.'

'I have a feeling that her desk might provide a clue.'

'Possibly. You must obtain a sight inside it.'

'That's easier said than done. How?'

'I'll think of a way,' Lander replied in an off-hand tone.

'I suppose it could conceal a radio transmitter, or something of the kind.'

'Perhaps, but that is not what we are after.' Observing Ainsworth's mystified expression, he added, 'The night air of Berlin is thick with transmissions from such sets. They can be easily monitored and are therefore not suitable for the passage of secret information. They serve a purpose for making contact but not much more.'

'I take it from that you already know whether Elli possesses such a set?'

'What we do know is that it isn't her normal way of passing information,' Lander said, in a tone which clearly indicated he wasn't prepared to disclose more. He looked grave. 'If you don't manage to make any progress this evening, we shall have to reconsider the whole position. As I said to you when you arrived the day before yesterday, time is of the essence.'

'I don't know what more I could have done,' Ainsworth said in a faintly nettled tone.

'Perhaps we expected too much,' Lander said, then throwing him a sudden smile added, 'But there's still this evening.' He paused. 'I think you should give thought to spending the night at her house.'

'And by that, I take it you're not suggesting a doss down on the sitting-room couch?'

'Correct, Mr. Ainsworth, I am not.'

The train pulled into a station and Lander rose. 'We get out here. It's the end of the line and we must change.'

'Where to now?'

'We'll take a train going South to Tempelhof. Have you travelled on that line yet?'

'No.'

'You'll find it interesting.'

'In what way?'

'For six stations it runs beneath the Eastern Sector of the city.'

They made their way in silence to another platform.

'Do you know who Elli's contacts in the east are?' Ainsworth asked while they were waiting for a train.

'Not specifically,' Lander replied in the tone Ainsworth was beginning to recognise as that employed when he didn't wish to be questioned about a particular subject. He lapsed into silence but then said suddenly, 'We knew nothing at all of her activities until recently, since when we've been working fast. We could pull her in any time except that we are very anxious to unravel the skein completely first. Otherwise, to change the metaphor, it's like cutting off the head of a worm. The rest wriggles away and a new head grows. We want to destroy the whole, and that's the only excuse for holding back. But it's a tricky business because every day that passes increases the chance of her taking flight.'

'Would that matter very much if you already know most things about her? After all, presumably she couldn't be used here again?'

'By the same token we shouldn't punish spies like Crofton, but should return them to their own countries?'

'It can be argued.'

'But not effectively. After all, when you lock up a spy in prison, you do it as much as anything to deter others. Without long sentences, there is no deterrent.'

A train came in and they boarded it. Shortly after it had pulled out of the next station but one, Lander said quietly, 'We're passing beneath the wall just about . . . now.'

Ainsworth experienced a small frisson and glanced quickly at his fellow passengers. The coach was only half-full. Opposite him sat a young girl, obviously a student, studying some pencilled notes in a thick exercise book. She wore a black sweater, bright-red skirt and black woollen stockings. Her hair was fair and long and her expression absorbed. Near her was an old woman with a bulging shopping bag on her lap who was staring stolidly in front of her. Farther along two men were reading newspapers and a youth was sitting head rested on hand and eyes focused on a thick tome which rested open on his lap. It suddenly struck him that no one was talking. The atmosphere resembled that in a 'plane as it accelerates down the runway for take-off.

The train slowed down and then at little more than walking pace passed through a station. The platform was lit by a single naked bulb, the exits were heavily wired and dust and debris everywhere lay thick. Standing in the shadows, only just discernible and watching the train pass was a young Vopo with a tommy-gun slung over his shoulder.

Ainsworth's mind was still dazed by the unearthliness of the scene when it was again repeated. The train slowed down once more to pass through another dead station. Dead but for the sinister figure who this time was standing so close to the edge of the platform that his nose almost touched the carriage windows.

To Ainsworth's surprise, the next station was brightly lit and the train halted. But no one alighted and there wasn't a soul on the platform to get in. A large melancholy-looking female in railway uniform signalled them on their way again.

'Friedrichstrasse Station,' Lander said. 'It's one of the control points for entering East Berlin.'

There followed three more disused stations, each with its grim reminder of the divided city which spread over their heads. Then abruptly they were back in the Western Sector and it seemed to Ainsworth that tension was palpably relaxed. The 'plane was safely airborne and safety belts could be unfastened.

'I shall get out at the next station,' Lander said. 'You ride on.'

'Do you wish me to alight at any particular station?' Ainsworth asked in an earnest tone, which immediately struck him as comical.

'It doesn't matter, provided we don't get out together. Give me a call at the same time tomorrow morning. Meanwhile, my fingers are crossed for this evening. It may be our last chance. . . .'

This enigmatic observation was left unexplained as the train then arrived at a station and Lander thrust his way out with most of the other passengers, who appeared to be changing on to another line. Ainsworth's last view of Lander as the train pulled out was of him trying to push his way past a solid block of people who were converging on a staircase.

Curious bloke, he reflected. As far as I'm concerned he doesn't have an existence outside our elaborately arranged encounters. He's undoubtedly intelligent and probably an admirable operator in his chosen field, but there's something faceless about him. If I were to meet him again in a month's time, as likely as not I'd fail to recognise him. This self-effacing quality may, of course, be one of his strongest assets, but it makes it impossible to envisage him in any other capacity than that in which I know him. Is he a thoughtful husband? Does he enjoy going to the cinema? What games does he play? Which is his favourite city? But no answers presented themselves, and at the next station Ainsworth alighted with Lander still in his mind as an efficient but insubstantial figure of the intelligence demi-monde.

He found himself not far from Tempelhof Airport and decided to pick up a taxi and return to the hotel. It was only just after eleven o'clock and he thought he would have an early light lunch somewhere on the Kurfürstendamm before deciding how to spend the afternoon. It was a warm, sunny day and a drive out to Wannsee, one of the attractive lakes within the confines of West Berlin, might be pleasant.

As he entered the hotel lobby, Fräulein Grimmer looked up from her inevitable ledger.

'Ach, Herr Ainsworth, your friend called but you were out,' she said in a chiding tone.

'My friend?'

She glanced at a piece of paper. 'Yes, Herr Jones. An English gentlemen.'

If Herr Jones was really English, it seemed likely his name was not that, and this feeling was confirmed by her answers to his following questions.

'What did he want?'

'He came for the package you had promised to leave for him,' she said sternly.

'I see. So what happened?'

'I told him you must have forgotten and he laughed and said, "he would"! Then he asked if someone could go and look in your bedroom to see if you had left it there.'

'And did someone?'

'I went myself, Herr Ainsworth.'

'But I'm afraid you didn't find the package.'

'No, but Herr Jones did,' she replied, with a triumphant glint in her eye.

'I don't follow.'

'I had only just got to your room—Herr Jones was with me—when I was called urgently to the telephone. Before I could re-join him, he had come downstairs again. He gave me back the key to your room and showed me the package. He had found it on the table. Luckily you had addressed it to him so he knew it was the right one.'

Ainsworth felt that his credulity had been stretched too far. Fräulein Grimmer herself was beginning to resemble one of Lewis Carroll's more grotesque creations as she recited events with evident self-satisfaction.

'But you never saw the package yourself?'

'Natürlich, Herr Jones showed it to me.'

'Fräulein Grimmer,' he said in a scything tone, 'I do not know a Mr. Jones, and I did not leave a package in my bedroom for him *or* anyone else.'

'But . . . but . . . I do not understand.'

'No more do I. But if you give me my key, I propose to find out exactly what has been going on.'

Leaving her looking like an exhausted fish, he ran up the stairs and along the corridor to his bedroom. At first glance, apart from the bed having been made, it looked no different from when he had gone out. Then he noticed that the book on the bedside table was now lying the wrong way up. This could, of course, have been the servant's doing. It was when he began opening drawers, however, that he knew someone had been through his possessions. One of his suitcases which he had left locked was still secured, though when he opened it it became apparent that the contents (his travel wallet containing his return ticket and a folder of travellers' cheques) had been shaken about.

He sat down on the edge of the bed and thought. Somebody had waited for him to leave the hotel and had then contrived to search his room. Who? And an even more compelling question, what had they been looking for?

Twice in recent years his London flat had been burgled and on each occasion he had regarded the intrusion of an unknown person into his home as much more disagreeable than the actual loss of possessions, a feeling which owed nothing to the fact that everything was insured anyway. He now experienced the same sensation as then, though much more sharply, for this intruder hadn't been looking for money or valuables. His search had been for information, and even at this moment he could be reporting results to those who had sent him. The results, Ainsworth knew, must have been negative for there was nothing the man could have found. To this extent, at least, he was living his part, that without opening up his head they'd find no give-away clues as to the reason for his presence in Berlin.

After a few minutes he went back downstairs where Fräulein Grimmer was still at the receipt of custom. He was pleased to observe her expression of faint anxiety when she saw him.

'Everything is now all right, Herr Ainsworth?' she asked hopefully.

He decided to go over to the offensive straight away. 'I am

surprised—astonished is perhaps the more appropriate word—
that you allow a stranger to enter one of your guests' bedrooms.
And not only allow, but actually escort him and leave him
there.'

She drew in her lips and tiny points of colour appeared on
each cheek.

'I explained, Herr Ainsworth, that I was called urgently to
the telephone otherwise I would not have left him there.'

'That still doesn't *satisfactorily* explain why you showed him
to my room in the first place.' She was about to protest, but he
went on, 'However, the damage has been done and there are
more important things to attend to. Firstly, what did this self-
claiming friend of mine look like?'

'He was not very tall and had a moustache,' she replied
suddenly.

'What colour was his hair?'

'Brown.'

'Fat or thin?'

'Neither, but in a few years perhaps he will be a little fat.'

'About how old?'

'Thirty-two to thirty-five.'

'How was he dressed?'

'He wore a grey suit and old suede shoes.'

'And you're sure he was British?'

'Jawohl. He spoke German well but with an accent. He was
most friendly,' she added.

'I'm sure he was.'

There was a silence before Fräulein Grimmer said in a steely
tone, 'If he was not your friend, why did he say he was and why
did he wish to go to your room?'

'You must work that out for yourself, Fräulein Grimmer.'

'If there is anything wrong going on, Herr Ainsworth, I must
ask——'

'Yes?'

'My hotel has a good name,' she said primly.

'I find that difficult to believe after this morning's experience.'

They were facing each other with implacable dislike across the
small desk and might so have remained but for the timely arrival of a new guest who came staggering through the front
door bearing two huge suitcases. Fräulein Grimmer immediately
gave him her attention and Ainsworth slipped away to go and

telephone Lander. An awkward impasse had been conveniently broken.

A female with a slight Cockney twang answered Lander's telephone.

'I'm afraid he's not in. Who's that speaking?'

'Martin Ainsworth.'

'Oh, it's Mr. Ainsworth! Shall I give Mr. Lander a message?'

'It doesn't matter. It can wait.'

'Forgive me questioning that, Mr. Ainsworth, but can it? If it was important enough for you to call, I'm sure Mr. Lander would wish to know what it's about as soon as possible.' In the brief silence which followed, she added, 'I know all about everything, Mr. Ainsworth, so you needn't be afraid to speak.'

'It's just this: that when I returned to my hotel in the middle of the morning, I found that my bedroom had been searched. Somebody called and was given access to it when he pretended to be a friend of mine.'

'I'll tell Mr. Lander that,' she remarked in a matter-of-fact tone. 'Did he find anything?'

'There was nothing *to* find.'

'No harm done then.'

'Except that I don't care for it.'

She laughed indulgently, as one who was accustomed to putting up with infinitely more trying circumstances.

· After he had rung off, he walked to one of the open-air cafés on the Kurfürstendamm and ordered a beer. The street was full of strolling people, as it seemed to be at all hours of the day and until late into the night, and he was again struck by the chic of the girls and the self-assured appearance of the young men. The wall and its environs, in reality so close to where he was sitting, could have belonged on a different planet. Buses and cars, all much newer looking than their counterparts in the Eastern Sector passed endlessly up and down, and in the background there was the intermittent rumble of the overhead railway which, with the U-Bahn, provided Berlin with as comprehensive a system of internal rail transportation as was enjoyed by any city in the world. Except that it was now two systems, rather as though the body's blood supply on one side was prevented by a severance of arteries from circulating on the other.

Ainsworth finished his beer and ordered another, together

with a ham omelette and a green salad. While he was waiting
for the food to come, his thoughts wandered to Crofton, sitting
in a prison cell, impassive and self-contained. It was Crofton
he had to thank for his present situation. A situation which he
felt sure his late client would have appreciated with sardonic
detachment. Perhaps Crofton's name should be his weapon this
coming evening. After all Bowes had said there was believed to
be some sort of connection between him and Elli, and there had
been something artificial about the way she had reacted when
he had casually introduced the name at their first meeting. And
thinking of names, what about von Sternmeier's? That was a
trump card he had temporarily overlooked.

When he had finished his meal, he decided to go and spend
an hour or so at the zoo, rather than make the excursion to the
lakes. Berlin's zoo had always been one of the city's meccas and,
though destroyed during the war, had been rebuilt and re-
stocked to the joy of its beleaguered citizens.

As he strolled along the broad, shady walks, he reflected idly
on the universal appeal of a zoo. And what was it that drew
humans of all ages to stand and stare with rapt absorption at the
antics of God's other creatures? Perhaps each acquired his own
particular satisfaction. As he watched three sea-lions swimming
with all the elegance of ballet dancers only to clamber ashore
with the ungainliness of fat old women with bad feet, Ainsworth
realised that for himself it was sheer wistful envy which filled
his mind. Each day was lived and enjoyed for itself. Problems
were dealt with as they arose and didn't fret the mind in expectation. Though what problems could beset a well-provided-
for sea-lion he couldn't imagine. Back to the simple, carefree
life, he thought with a sigh as he turned into the insect house
to be repelled by the sheer evil of most of its denizens. If there
was anything carefree about a scorpion or a black widow
spider, it remained one of Providence's better-kept secrets.

He walked back to the hotel feeling that he had had an
entertaining afternoon, confused only by his attempt to discern
answers to the complicated human situation in what he had
seen. Perhaps he should have suggested a rendezvous there with
Elli.

He lay on his bed and read for a couple of hours, then
showered and changed and set out for Dahlem in a taxi. As
he handed in his key, he said with unmistakable meaning, 'I

am not expecting anyone to call, while I'm out, Fräulein Grimmer.'

She made no reply, but folded her lips in a disapproving expression and turned to an abrupt study of the ever-open ledger on the desk.

Elli had insisted that they should meet at the restaurant and he had accepted this without argument, though he expected another tussle when it came to seeing her home at the end of the evening. The restaurant was about fifteen minutes' walk from her house and he arrived ahead of time. It was one of those establishments with a low ceiling and just sufficient light to distinguish fork from spoon. As far as Ainsworth could tell, none of its tables was occupied. No wonder Elli had suggested meeting there. It was every spy's dream-place of assignation.

He had just ordered himself a Scotch on the rocks when she arrived.

'So you found your way all right, Martin?' she said, proffering her cheek for a kiss. 'And what have you been doing today?' she went on as he helped her into her chair and looked round for the bar-waiter.

'I went to the zoo.'

'I adore the zoo,' she exclaimed eagerly. 'You know it is all new since you were here? And what else have you done?'

There was something puzzling about her mood. After last night's events, he had thought there might be a further degree of restraint between them, but instead she was bubbling over with friendly interest. Almost, compulsively so.

'Nothing else today,' he replied. 'I read quite a bit.'

'But, Martin, there is so much for you to see. You should not waste your time reading, you can do that at home.' She took a sip of her cocktail, then putting down the glass with elaborate care, she turned her gaze full on him. 'Martin, what is the real reason for your coming to Berlin? Tell me the truth!'

He was glad that years spent in the courts had taught him how to mask his emotions and that he was able to answer Elli with more composure than he felt.

'I don't know what you mean, Elli, I have told you the truth. I'd been meaning to come for several years and here I am.'

'But what made you come *now*?'

'Principally, because I hadn't made plans to go anywhere else during the summer vacations. I imagine everyone has something which they are always going to do one day but never get round to—or at any rate something which gets put off year by year before it is achieved. My trip here is in that category.'

'Am I anything to do with your coming, Martin?' she asked quietly.

Everything was the true answer, though he realised that this would not only be ambiguous but doubly perilous. Instead he said, 'Finding you has made all the difference to my visit, Elli.'

'And yet you waited until you arrived to get in touch with me,' she said, still searching his face with disconcerting intensity.

'I explained that to you, too. It could have happened that I might have rung your bell and run away before you opened the door.'

'But it did not happen like that, and now you are asking me to go back to England to stay with you.'

'Yes,' he replied in a puzzled tone.

'Because you are in love with me?'

'Because seeing you again has made me realise how fond of you I still am.'

He began to feel wretchedly uncomfortable, and his mind was filled with silent curses against Bowes and Lander for having led him along the path of such odious deception. Even though Elli were a Communist spy, she remained a woman with a heart. Why had he ever allowed himself to be sucked into this grubby world of duplicity, where the means were always held to justify the end.

'How much longer are you staying?' she asked abruptly.

'Probably not more than a couple of days. Why?'

'I just wondered how much time I had to make up my mind about your invitation.'

'You mean . . .'

'Perhaps I shall come with you, Martin, after all.'

'Oh, my God, what on earth do I say now?' was all that his brain managed to transmit in silent panic.

'You were right, the school could look after itself for a few weeks and I should love to see England again.'

'You'll definitely come?' he asked in what to his ears sounded like a desperate croak.

She nodded her head. 'That is, if the invitation is still open?'

'Of course it is.' He looked round for a waiter. 'We must drink to this, Elli,' he said. The Security Service had got him into this, the same could get him out. 'I am so glad,' he went on, staunchly, 'because last night you seemed full of anxiety and secret fears and . . . well'—he laughed disarmingly—'I was sure you were mixed up in one of these shady organisations which Berlin is said to spawn. Why *were* you so mysterious last night, Elli?'

Even as he asked the question, his brain seemed suddenly to clear and he kicked himself for being an unbelievable fool, of course, she had no intention of coming to England. She was acting on orders to call his bluff. That was it and he had almost fallen. He kicked himself again for being so naïve, though he felt considerably more cheerful now that he realised she had been playing a part. It made it much easier to play his.

'I was tired and jumpy last night,' she said in a dismissive tone. 'Berlin has that effect every so often.'

'I'm not surprised, living as you do a hundred miles behind the iron curtain and literally surrounded by barbed wire. That's why it'll do you good to get out of the city. We'll leave the day after tomorrow. I'll make our reservations in the morning.' He bent over the menu which lay in front of him. 'But before we go any further, let's order.'

He decided, while they were waiting for their food, to steer the conversation towards more general topics, and used Elli's supposed forthcoming visit to England as an excuse for discoursing on the change of scene which would greet her. London's new sky-line and the city's festering traffic problems, though capable of evoking strong emotions at home, were scarcely likely to do so in Berlin. In the event Elli listened with a detachment which hardly seemed to accord with her expressed eagerness to come and see for herself. She might have been someone listening to a description of life on Mars whose own horizon didn't stretch beyond Margate.

A little later while they ate and talked he tried to analyse his true feelings towards her. He had been pretending so hard that he hadn't paused to find out what lay beneath the veneer. Twenty-five years ago he had wanted to marry her, and but for Hitler starting a war would probably have done so. Now? Well, he wasn't sure that he wanted to marry anyone and anyway he was far too enslaved by social convention to run off with a Communist spy. But supposing Elli was just Elli and not an agent of the East German government, what then? To what extent in fact did his knowledge of her influence his feelings? He glanced at her covertly as she bent over her plate to remove bones from the fish she was eating. How much of the earlier Elli remained? And anyway what was it about her that had made him feel like Don Juan and the reluctant dragon rolled into one? It was difficult to recall and pinpoint such indefinables. She was still good to look at and there was still the occasional fleeting expression which once upon a time had melted his insides. He was sitting back, watching her wrestling with a fish bone and reflecting on the strange chemistry which draws two people together when quite suddenly an expression of such pathetic, childlike vulnerability possessed her features that his heart could have burst. Considerably shaken he turned quickly away and gave his attention to the pork chop on the plate in front of him.

During a pause over coffee, Elli said, 'I think I have remembered the name of Wolfgang's friend. Did you mean Gustav von Sternmeier?'

'That's the fellow. As a matter of fact I recalled his name after leaving you last night. What happened to him?'

She shook her head. 'I've no idea. He disappeared shortly after Wolfgang was arrested and I haven't heard of him since.' With a resigned shrug she added, 'He probably died during the war.'

Clever of her to mention his name, he thought. She obviously guessed I'd remember it sooner or later and decided to remove the sting by getting in first.

Unlike the previous evening she seemed in no hurry to leave, and Ainsworth began to wonder if she was deliberately prolonging the occasion for some reason. Her conversation was chiefly about the sufferings of Germany during and after the war and the current lack of sympathy amongst West Germans for their brethren in Berlin.

'They would sooner not know about us,' she declared bitterly. 'We are on their conscience and of course nobody likes to be reminded of their conscience. In England I believe you have some expression about *Jack*?'

'I'm all right Jack?'

'Yes. That expresses the attitude of many West Germans towards us Berliners. The politicians talk a lot about reuniting our country, but everyone knows it will not happen in the foreseeable future without a miracle.'

'Surely the fact that the Bonn government pours millions of marks into West Berlin demonstrates their concern and awareness of the situation.'

'It is like, perhaps, Martin, when you have a black sheep in your family. He is a nuisance and you don't wish to be reminded too often of his existence because that is inconvenient. Nevertheless, you arrange for your bank to send him some money each month, because otherwise he is on your conscience. We are on the conscience. We are on the conscience of the free world and in particular of our own German brothers in the Federal Republic.'

'And what about your brothers in the Democratic Republic on the other side of the wall?' he asked dryly.

She gave him a sharp look. 'To them West Berlin is a symbol of hope,' she replied as though repeating a well-worn slogan. The only thing is, it's not her slogan, Ainsworth reflected.

It was after eleven o'clock before Elli glanced at her watch and, smothering a yawn, said, 'It has been a lovely evening,' Martin.'

'No headache tonight?' he asked with a smile. 'I'll tell the head waiter to get us a taxi.'

'I would like to walk. It is not far and the air is nice at this hour.'

'Let's do that.'

As they left the restaurant, she slipped her arm through his and pressed herself close against his side.

'We can go through the little park here,' she said, leading him along a footpath which ran off between trees. 'It is a short cut.'

It struck Ainsworth that she might be leading him straight into an ambush, but there was little he could do about it other than sharpen his senses. The path came out into the open and wound round the rim of a sunken lake. He started suddenly at the sound of movement off to their right in some bushes.

'Lovers,' Elli said laconically. 'In the summer the parks are full of them at night. Also in London, I expect.'

'And in every other city inhabited by both sexes,' he remarked with a light laugh.

He was almost surprised when they reached the road on the far side of the park without anything untoward happening. They turned right and then left.

'Now we are in Karolinerstrasse,' Elli announced. 'It is very quiet round here at nights.'

'So I've noticed.'

There were indeed neither cars nor pedestrians about and most of the houses appeared dark and unoccupied. People must either go to bed very early or stay out very late. He was about to ask which when he saw that they'd arrived at number fourteen. Elli took care to ensure he wasn't able to watch her unlock the front gate, though unlike the previous evening she obviously expected—wanted—him to come into the house. Closing the gate behind him, he followed her up to the door which she had opened.

He was directly behind her as she entered the living-room and put a hand out to the light switch. In the next instant he heard her gasp of fear and at the self-same moment he saw the body sprawled downwards on the carpet.

MARTIN AINSWORTH had seen quite a few dead people in his time, including a number who had died violently, but there was something particularly dramatic about the position of the body which lay on Elli's sitting-room floor. It might almost have been arranged for an interesting camera shot in a murder film. One arm was outflung, the other lay beneath the body. The legs, bent slightly at the knees, were together and one foot lay on top of the other. The face was completely obscured from view.

Even as he stepped past Elli, Ainsworth saw the ugly, reddish-brown stain on the carpet a few inches from the man's head. He bent down and rather gingerly turned the head in order to learn more.

The man had been neatly shot between the eyes and blood was still seeping sluggishly from the hole. Indeed, Ainsworth had noticed that the body was still warm as soon as he touched it. Despite the now grotesque appearance of the face, he had no difficulty in recognising it as that of Koeslin, the student from Elli's school.

He looked up and observed that Elli had also seen who it was.

'We'd better ring the police,' he said quietly. He realised afterwards that he had spoken instinctively and with temporary forgetfulness of their situation.

'Yes, I will do it,' she replied in an abstracted voice. 'But you must go first, Martin. It will not be good if you are here when they come.'

'Why on earth not?'

'You are a foreigner and they might make difficulties.'

'That's crazy! I can't possibly leave you alone with a dead body. Of course I must stay.'

'No, Martin, please go! I shall be all right. I can explain everything to them. There will be no need to mention you.'

'I'm not worried about being mentioned. And anyway, what exactly will you say to them?'

'I shall tell them that I came home and found Herr Koeslin lying there.'

Ainsworth once more had the feeling that he was swimming against a strong undercurrent. Elli was determined, for some reason or other, to get him out of the house. Well, he was equally determined to stay.

'What was he doing here and how did he get in?' He glanced round the room and back at Elli.

'The police will find out.'

'Well, you go and 'phone them and I'll have a look around.' Before Elli had time to reply, he walked out of the room to begin an exploratory tour of the rest of the house. When five minutes later he returned, she was sitting on the arm of a chair staring at the floor near Koeslin's feet.

'There's no sign of his having broken in,' he announced. 'All windows and doors are still secure. Have you 'phoned the police?'

'Not yet,' she answered in a quietly stubborn voice.

'Has he ever been to the house before?' She shook her head. 'What could have brought him here, Elli? You must have some idea.'

In view of everything else, it didn't surprise him that after an initial shock, Elli had shown no more agitation than someone finding a spider in the bath. He realised, however, that to tackle her along that line would achieve nothing.

'Shall I 'phone the police?' he asked.

'No. I will, after you have gone.'

'Why are you so anxious for me to leave?'

'I've told you, Martin. They can make difficulties for foreigners. You would have to stay in Berlin perhaps, and it could be very inconvenient for you to alter all your plans. For me it is different, and I know there will be no trouble, so you need not worry, Martin.'

'You're quite certain you'll be able to manage?' he asked, with apparent reluctance.

'Yes, I promise I shall be all right.'

'I still think,' he remarked doubtfully, 'that you underestimate the problem of explaining to the police how you happen upon a dead body in your house. But if you really think they could make difficulties for me . . .'

'I know them, Martin,' she said vehemently. 'They could.'

He forebore to ask why police, who could apparently become so unreasonable on finding a foreigner at the scene of a crime, should be painted in such accommodating colours where one of their own nationals was concerned. Let her believe that he had swallowed the inconsistency.

With a final glance at the body, he went out into the hall, followed by Elli. Her relief at his departure was apparent. As he kissed her good night, he felt certain of one thing only, namely that she had no intention of 'phoning the police.

'Don't hesitate to call me at the hotel if you have any trouble, and I'll come straight back,' he said earnestly.

'That is sweet of you, Martin, but everything will be all right. I will telephone you in the morning to show you that I have not been arrested.'

The front gate buzzed open as he reached it, and they exchanged waves before he walked off along the dimly-lit road. He went as far as the corner, then crossed quickly to the other side and, keeping well into the shadows, walked back until he was opposite the house. The large tree which had afforded cover to the mysterious person who had observed his departure that first evening now offered him similar service.

He looked at his watch and saw that it was five minutes before midnight. The only sounds were of distant traffic on the Clay Allee and, much nearer, of a precocious nightingale. Compelled to listen to it, he decided that its song was considerably overrated. Like bagpipes, it needed to be heard at a distance. The one sound which was most obviously missing was that of arriving police cars and ambulances.

As he stared across at the house, a light suddenly came on in Elli's bedroom and he saw her come to the window and draw the curtains. A minute or two later the light went off again. When, after a further five minutes, nothing more had happened, he decided that the time for action had arrived.

The front gate was locked and its mechanism controlled from inside the house: the fence either side of it wasn't merely six feet high, but topped by unfriendly-looking spikes. In the circumstances he had decided that his best hope was to try to enter from the next-door garden, and with this in mind he now walked twenty yards back along the pavement, then looking in either direction like an over-cautious pedestrian, he darted across the road and into the shadows on the other side.

The house next to Elli's was larger, and bounded by a low brick wall. But there seemed no point in clambering over even low walls if the gate could be opened. It could, and he quickly moved into the shadow of a tree growing in the garden to the right of the house, which was itself in complete darkness. A path ran round the side of the garage and he soon found himself at the back of the house. It was much darker here without any reflected light from street lamps, and he paused to get his bearings.

Walking on tip-toe, he made his way first to the end of the garden, and then across to the fence which divided it from Elli's. Twice he plunged into soft earth, on the second occasion to be scratchily embraced by a rose bush. If they found his footprints the next morning, it was just too bad. It certainly wasn't worth while trying to obliterate them.

He now found himself up against a stout, wood paling fence, with shrubs and bushes on either side. At least it was a foot less high than that which bounded the pavement. Choosing the point at which he would cross, he set off back down the garden to where he had noticed a pile of logs. Six of these provided an adequate, if precarious, platform from which to launch himself over the fence. He landed in a compost heap on the other side and paused to regain his breath before emerging from the cover of the bushes.

When he did so, it was to find himself on a strip of side lawn no more than fifteen yards from the house, and looking straight at the sitting-room windows. Though the curtains were drawn, he could see that the light was still on and it was possible there'd be a chink through which he could discover what was happening inside.

Moving with great stealth, he crept over until he was standing right outside the window, only there to find that the curtains completely obscured all view. He tried putting his head against the wall beside the window and discovered he had an extremely narrow and oblique view into the room. It was like seeing the new moon when you wanted the whole face.

While he was peering, a shadow was suddenly thrown on to the strip of wall which lay at the end of his gaze. It remained only a few seconds and then maddeningly slid off like a lantern slide. It had been time enough, however, for him to realise that it didn't belong to Elli. The owner of the shadow had been smoking and Elli didn't smoke.

Excitedly, he pressed his ear against the side of the window, but could hear nothing. The back door suddenly opened and somebody stepped out into the small, cemented area, where he'd noticed a refuse bin. He couldn't see what was happening and he dare not move, since whoever it was was only just round the corner from where he stood.

Then, as the person moved back inside the house, he heard Elli's voice say in German, 'I wish they'd hurry up and come.'

A second later the door was closed and Ainsworth decided to retire to the cover of the bushes and await events. This time *he* would be the silent observer of Elli's visitors, and he felt himself tingling with expectation. He was more than ever certain that whoever it was that Elli wished would hurry up and come, would not turn out to be the police. But as much as he wished to see who was about to arrive, he wanted even more to know who was already inside, for they must have been there when he and Elli arrived back from the restaurant. It was just possible that someone could have entered while he was in the next-door garden, but it seemed much more likely that they had been in the house all along. And if this was so, then the inference must be that it was the person who had shot Koeslin. But what had Koeslin been doing there anyway, and who was he? Clearly he was not the student of her school as Elli had made out—or at least not primarily that.

While his thoughts were revolving round these questions like a dog trying unsuccessfully to catch its tail, he suddenly heard a car approaching. The engine was turned off while it was still fifty yards away, and the only sound was of the wheels crunching small pebbles and sticks in the gutter as it came to a halt in front of the house. Only by listening intently did he hear anyone get out and close the door with great quietness. As yet he was unable to see anything, but suddenly the front gate opened with its tiny buzz and two figures stepped inside and walked swiftly up to the front door, which opened as they reached it. A second later it closed and they'd been swallowed up.

Apart from the fact they were men and they were hatless and coatless, he had not been able to distinguish anything. It was important to move into a position from which he could observe the front door when they came out again. His best hope of seeing anything was in the light reflected from the hall. Peering through the front fence, he saw that the vehicle was a small van. He could only glimpse the top half from where he stood, and realised that he would not be able to take its number without returning to the road, which was scarcely a practical proposition at the moment.

He must have waited twenty minutes before anything further happened, and by this time was beginning to feel that he could have chosen ten better vantage points than the one he had actually selected. He was on the point of creeping across to the sitting-room window to take another oblique squint round the end of the curtains when the hall light suddenly went out and the front door opened. Straining his eyes until they ached, he was able to make out two figures emerging carrying a heavy bundle between them. At least there was no doubt as to what that must be.

A third person now came out of the house and, brushing past them, went and held open the gate. All three then disappeared from his view and he heard the van's doors being softly opened and closed. A second later its engine sprang to life with a staccato noise which rent the stillness of the night and the van was driven off. The gate was now pushed open and the third person re-appeared and walked back into the house.

Though Ainsworth had been unable to see his face, there had been something vaguely familiar about the shape of the head, and more particularly about the gait, as the figure had passed to and fro through the luminous night. Surely there couldn't be another with that distinctive corkscrew roll. The more he thought about it, the more certain he became that it was none other than Gustav von Sternmeier, who had just entered the house. Gustav von Sternmeier whom Elli had airily dismissed only an hour or so before as having most probably died during the war.

The most vital thing now was to return to his observation post on the other side of the road, for then he'd not only be able to see von Sternmeier's departure, but also follow him.

Remounting the fence was less easy since there was nothing handy on which to stand. It meant a leap, a clamber and a fall the other side. He was glad that he still occasionally jumped a tennis net out of sheer exuberance to show that he could, and though the paling fence was a more formidable obstacle, a good spring was necessary to both feats.

Landing beside his platform of logs, he brushed himself down and decided that he might as well return them to their pile on his way out. The house was still in darkness, though this was hardly surprising seeing that it was getting on for one o'clock.

When he arrived back in the shadow of the tree opposite Elli's house, he was relieved to see that the sitting-room light was still on, for this meant that von Sternmeier was most probably still inside. Once the downstairs lights were extinguished and those in the bedroom came on, it would mean either that von Sternmeier had departed while Ainsworth was negotiating the fence or that he was stopping the night. He glanced at his watch and decided to give it half an hour before throwing in his hand and making his own way to bed.

In fact he did not have to wait as long, for the front door suddenly opened and closed, the gate gave its little buzz, and von Sternmeier was striding down the Karolinerstrasse with Ainsworth flitting from tree to tree along the opposite side of the street. Only once when he accidentally kicked a stone and sent it clattering into the road did his quarry look round. Immediately afterwards his pace quickened and Ainsworth, whose stride was a good deal shorter, felt himself skimming along like a ballet dancer.

Dahlem Dorf underground station was clearly von Sternmeier's objective, and Ainsworth wondered if the trains still ran at this hour. They emerged into the main road near the station and von Sternmeier crossed to the far side from the entrance. There was a car parked, and almost before Ainsworth realised what had happened, he had got in and it had driven off. As it pulled away, he saw that it was a taxi. There wasn't another in sight.

Before he reached the station, he could see that it was closed. So there he was, no cabs, no trains, no buses and about five miles from his hotel. There seemed no alternative but to walk. Happily it was a nice night, though as he set out he reflected that he could have done without further exercise.

It was a quarter to three when he arrived back at the Hotel Lübeck to find its street door firmly bolted in his face. After rattling it several times, he put his finger on the bell-push and kept it there for a full minute. At length he heard someone coming down the stairs, followed by bolts being pulled back. When the door did open it was to reveal Fräulein Grimmer in night-attire which included a sort of mop cap on her head.

'I'm sorry to get you out of bed,' he said in a tone which belied the words.

'Guests are requested to notify late returns so that arrangements can be made,' she replied nastily. 'There is a notice in your bedroom and perhaps you would read it, Herr Ainsworth.'

'I didn't expect to be so late. I'm sorry.'

She looked him up and down and her expression became more disdainful, but apart from a stiff 'good night', she said nothing further. When he reached his room and saw himself in the mirror, he understood why her disapproval had increased as he'd come into the light, for he looked exactly like someone who had spent the evening clambering over fences and concealing himself in bushes. His face was streaked with dirt and his suit heavily rumpled. The surprising thing was that she had let him in at all.

As he undressed, he felt completely wide awake and even regretted the necessity of having to go to bed. Elli had promised she would telephone him in the morning to reassure him about her encounter with the police, and he could hardly wait to receive her call. And if it didn't come through, he'd ring her.

He wondered how the anonymous Lander would react to his report of the evening's events. It was time he did something more than coax and chivvy other people over the telephone and furtively make trips on the underground.

As he switched out the light and let his head sink back into the creamily soft pillow, he made up his mind that in the unlikely event of Her Majesty's Security Service ever again wanting to use him, they'd have to bait the trap a good deal better next time. He drifted off to sleep trying to picture James Bond in Fräulein Grimmer's establishment.

Later, however, he dreamt not of Bond but of the dead Koeslin lying on Elli's floor and of the very much alive von Sternmeier.

THE maid in the dining-room looked at him with new interest when Ainsworth sat down at breakfast the next morning. He had clearly gained in stature in her eyes whatever the tale Fräulein Grimmer had been putting around in the kitchen. She insisted on pouring out his coffee for him and later retired to a position from which she could keep him under ceaseless appraisal.

Since he was late for breakfast and had only managed to beat Fräulein Grimmer's clock by a few minutes, he half-expected that Elli's call would come through while he was at table. That she would telephone him he had not the slightest doubt since she would obviously regard it as very important to reassure him that all was well and that she had had no trouble in explaining matters to the police.

However, she hadn't rung by the time he had finished his meal and since it was nearly ten o'clock and time to make his daily call to Lander he left a message that anyone 'phoning him should be told that he'd be back in twenty minutes.

He selected one of the call boxes at the Zoo Station and dialled Lander's number. Normally it was answered promptly but this morning it rang for half a minute before the girl with the slight Cockney twang came on the line.

'No, I'm afraid Mr. Lander's had to go out,' she said in what Ainsworth thought was a mildly-agitated voice. 'Something rather important has just broken,' she added with a nervous catch.

'Did he leave any message for me?'

'No, but I know he'll be getting in touch with you, Mr. Ainsworth, just as soon as he can.'

'I dare say, but I have something important to tell him. What do you suggest I do?'

'He'll be calling the office in the course of the morning and I'll give him your message. Can you go back and wait at your hotel?'

'I'll stay in till eleven o'clock,' Ainsworth replied, 'but after that I shall be going out.'

'I'll tell Mr. Lander.'

'You sound in a bit of a state this morning,' he said amiably.

She gave a nervous laugh. 'Oh, we have these alarms from time to time.'

'Is it anything to do with the matter I'm interested in?'

He could almost hear the shutter coming down on her voice. 'I'm afraid it's nothing I can discuss on the telephone. If you'll excuse me, Mr. Ainsworth, I think there's someone at the door. . . .'

'All right, goodbye, Miss . . .'

'Smith.'

'. . . Miss Smith, goodbye.'

When he arrived back at the hotel and learnt that no one had telephoned while he'd been out, he decided to ring Elli himself. He did so, but got no reply. Presumably she was at the school. When he rang there, however, it was to have an unintelligible conversation in which neither party understood the other and to be left hanging on until the line resolved the matter itself by going dead. It seemed clear that it was going to be one of those days which assume the quality of a bad dream as one frustration follows another.

He decided that if Lander hadn't got in touch with him by eleven o'clock, he would take a taxi to Elli's school at Dahlem and seek her out. His professed anxiety for her safety provided him with as good a reason as he could have for suddenly turning up there.

No call came through, and as he handed in his key to Fräulein Grimmer, who was radiating an aura of massive disapproval behind her desk, he said, 'A Mr. Lander may telephone. Will you tell him I'll be in about two o'clock?'

'You won't be in to lunch then?' she replied frigidly.

'No.'

'I'll inform the dining-room.'

'Please do!'

'There's a notice in your bedroom about letting the management know in good time if you're going to be out for a meal,' she said with asperity.

'I think the man you admitted to my bedroom yesterday must have made off with all the notices.'

She folded her lips and took refuge in the ledger, and Ainsworth sauntered forth in search of a taxi.

The ride to Dahlem took about fifteen minutes, and the driver appeared to know exactly where the school was.

It turned out to be housed in a large, grey, pseudo-Gothic villa which was much in need of a coat of paint. The road in which it stood was not far from American army headquarters and a vast radio mast towered over the area. It looked formidable enough to pluck signals from anywhere out of the ether and return them with interest over the moon.

Ainsworth paid off the taxi and walked up the short drive. He could see a classful of students in the room to the right of the front-door, but no sign of Elli there.

A withered old man came to the door in answer to the bell, and Ainsworth guessed that it was he who had also answered the telephone. No wonder it had been such a sterile experience. The old boy looked about a hundred and was dressed in the remains of some sort of uniform—possibly he'd been Bismarck's batman—and a pair of white canvas shoes.

'I'd like to speak to Frau Seidler,' he said in German.

'Nicht hier heute,' the old man mumbled.

'Where is Frau Seidler today?'

'Nicht hier.'

'Do you know where I can find her?'

'Nicht hier,' he repeated, shaking his head vigorously.

'Was geht, Fritz?'

At the sound of another voice, Ainsworth glanced up and saw a woman coming towards them from the back of the hall. She had very black hair cut like a Japanese doll's, her face was white, as was her blouse, her skirt and stockings and shoes were black. She also wore a pair of heavy, black-rimmed spectacles.

The old man gestured in Ainsworth's direction and said something which he didn't understand. The black and white female now said in English, 'I am Frau Frings. I am Frau Seidler's assistant. Can I help you?'

'My name's Martin Ainsworth, and I'm an old friend of Frau Seidler's. I gather she is not here today?'

'No, Herr Ainsworth, I'm afraid she is away.'

'That's funny,' he said, in a genuinely puzzled tone. 'I was dining with her only last night and she didn't mention that she was going away.'

'It was very sudden. Her aunt was taken ill in the night.'

'Her aunt?'

'Yes. She has gone to visit her sick aunt.' As said by Frau Frings it sounded like a sentence off the blackboard in one of her classrooms.

'Have you seen Frau Seidler this morning?'

'No. She telephoned me.'

'Did she mention where her aunt lived?'

'It is her aunt in Hanover.'

'How long will she be away?'

'A few days, perhaps.' Frau Frings, who had shown signs of becoming restive under this cross-examination, now said, 'If you will excuse me, my class is waiting.'

'Yes, of course. Thank you for your help. I will write to Frau Seidler. Do you happen to know her aunt's address?'

'No.'

As Ainsworth walked away from the house, he felt Frau Frings' eyes burning his back. He turned his head when he reached the gate and was just in time to see her close the front door.

It now seemed more important than ever that he should get in touch with Lander, and he strode off in the direction of a café, which he remembered the taxi having passed at the top of the road, and where there would be a telephone.

It was empty and, to appease the proprietor, he ordered a coffee before making the call. Though he let the number ring for half a minute, there was no reply. Presumably Lander wasn't yet back and the Cockney secretary had gone off to an early lunch. Nevertheless, it seemed odd that the office should be left unattended, and it was certainly beyond coincidence that his flurry of activity followed so soon on events at Elli's house. After a few seconds' thought, he dialled the number of his hotel.

'Hotel Lübeck,' Fräulein Grimmer answered primly.

'Mr. Ainsworth speaking. Have there been any telephone calls for me?'

'Ja. Herr Lander.'

'How long ago?'

'Five minutes.'

'Did he leave any message?'

'He will 'phone again later, Herr Ainsworth.'

'Did he say when?'

'This afternoon. I told him you would be back at two o'clock.'

'Did he say where he was speaking from?'

'I did not ask him such questions,' Fräulein Grimmer retorted.

'If he calls again will you please ask him how I can get in touch with him?'

He left the café and decided that since he was in the area, he would go to 14 Karolinerstrasse, and see if anyone was at the house.

But this time the front gate failed to buzz open when he rang the bell, and the place had a generally shut-up appearance. So far as he could see all the windows were closed and the curtains in the sitting-room were pulled partially across. It seemed that Elli really had made an abrupt departure, though scarcely to visit a sick aunt in Hanover. It was much more likely she was now ensconced somewhere on the east side of the wall. The one thing Bowes and Lander had feared had come about, namely she had taken fright and fled. This looked like the conclusion of his assignment.

Staring now at her villa, it was difficult to realise that it was just about twelve hours since they had returned to find Koeslin's body. Who was he? And what had happened to his corpse? It seemed much more likely that it had been unceremoniously dumped in a canal than that it had been accorded Christian burial. Perhaps it, too, was now in East Berlin. There was something completely macabre about the whole episode which made Ainsworth give an involuntary shudder as he began to walk away from the house.

He had not gone more than a few yards when a car passed him and pulled up outside the house opposite Elli's. It had American Army plates and Ainsworth, who had paused to stare, saw a man in officer's uniform get out. While the man was locking the driver's door, he crossed the road and went over to him.

'Excuse me,' he said, with a hopeful smile, 'but I wonder if you have any idea what's happened to Frau Seidler who lives opposite at number fourteen? I was expecting to find her in, but the whole place seems shut up and I can't get an answer.'

The man whom he was addressing was around thirty, and had a pleasant, open face. He wore the badges of the rank of a captain.

'Are you British, sir?'

'That's right. My name's Ainsworth.'

'Pleased to know you, Mr. Ainsworth. Mine's Kramer. As to Frau Seidler, well I didn't even know her name, until you mentioned it. We've only been living in this house for three weeks and we haven't gotten round to knowing our neighbours.' He seemed to be trying to make up his mind about something and gave Elli's house a long, hard stare. 'Though as a matter of fact,' he went on slowly after a long pause, 'I think I can answer your question.' His uncomfortably steady gaze became refocused on Ainsworth's face. 'It so happens that one of our kids woke up about five o'clock this morning and was crying. After I'd seen to him and was about to return to bed, I heard a car pull up outside. I went across to the window, that one up there'—he pointed in the direction—'and was just in time to see Frau Seidler—is that her name?—come down the path with a couple of bags and get into the car. I guess she must have been waiting for him, since he'd scarcely halted before she was out of the house. He never even switched off the engine.'

'You couldn't see who the driver was?'

'As far as I was concerned he was just a guy behind a steering-wheel. I'm afraid I'm not at my most observant at five o'clock in the morning.'

Ainsworth grinned. 'I suppose she must have been called hurriedly.'

'Very hurriedly, I'd guess,' Kramer said, dryly. 'Forgive my asking, but do you know her well, Mr. Ainsworth?'

'I've known her a long time, but until this week I hadn't seen her for years. I happened to be in Berlin and looked her up again.'

'I see,' Kramer said thoughtfully. Then after a pause: 'May I enquire what she does?'

'She runs a language school not far from here.'

'Is that so!' Something was clearly troubling him and Ainsworth waited hopefully. 'I'd been wondering . . .' His thoughts appeared to trail away with the sentence.

'She's someone who's inclined to keep herself to herself,' Ainsworth said gratuitously.

Kramer gave him another appraising stare, then looking back at Elli's house, said slowly, 'My wife and I have wondered . . . Once or twice, there's been . . . how shall I say it . . . well, nocturnal comings and goings. Not every night, but they've been more frequent of late. And then just the other evening, my wife was certain she saw someone keeping watch in the shadow of this tree. I was out at the time, but I've told her if it happens again to call me. She's not a nervous person, Mr. Ainsworth, but that upset her. And it set us wondering what went on opposite.'

Ainsworth shook his head in puzzled sympathy. 'Frau Seidler's a widow, but I don't know much about her present way of life. I understood from what she told me that she lived pretty quietly.'

'Oh, she doesn't throw noisy parties or anything like that. It's just that there've been these rather shadowy flittings around her house.' He seemed about to add something further, but after studying the ground with a thoughtful expression he looked up abruptly and said, 'I must go inside, Mr. Ainsworth, or my wife'll wonder what's happened to me.'

'Well, thanks anyway for what you've told me. I'll try 'phoning Frau Seidler later in the day. She may be back then.'

Kramer pursed his lips and gave Ainsworth a small, speculative nod.

So Elli had decamped at five o'clock in the morning, ostensibly to hurry to the bedside of her sick aunt in Hanover. Koeslin's death had obviously precipitated a crisis and everyone had gone to ground. Ainsworth imagined that this must be a fairly frequent occurrence amongst the field operators in the espionage business.

He began to wonder incredulously whether his own intervention might not have contributed in some way to the events of the past twenty-four hours. To what extent had the innocent spy at large flurried the professional dovecotes? It was only a short step to start pondering the safety of his own position.

When he reached the U-Bahn Station he found himself giving careful scrutiny to the other travellers, and when the train came in, he chose the carriage which had the most people in it. There must be safety in numbers, even in this city of mysterious disappearances.

For the first time, since he had set off on this mad assignment, he felt out of his depth and distinctly apprehensive.

'Come and see me in my office, please, Comrade Fröhlich.'
'Jawohl, Comrade Grossman.'
The chilly voice, the formal address all indicated to Fröhlich

that Erika Grossman was in a disagreeable mood. Presumably the minister had been on her tail again. That always upset her and she never lost any time in passing his harsh words down the line. Fröhlich sighed. The trouble was having a woman in such a senior post. They just didn't have the right temperament for the upper echelons of intelligence work. Erika was a dedicated member of the party, she was courageous, she had a subtle mind, but she also had her limitations which mostly sprang from the fact of her sex. She didn't know how to treat subordinates, nor could she stand up to her superiors—at least not to one as abrasively unpleasant as the comrade minister.

Fröhlich knocked on her door and this time waited before turning the handle.

'Herein.' She was standing with her back to the window, her feet apart, her hands clasped behind her back. She could have been either an admiral on his quarter-deck, or a headmaster about to flog and expel some miscreant. 'The comrade minister is very displeased about the Dahlem operation,' she said before he'd even closed the door behind him. 'He is asking for a full report.'

'Naturally, he is entitled to one.'

Erika Grossman frowned. 'I don't think you realise how seriously the matter is regarded, Comrade Fröhlich.'

'Indeed I do, but these things happen in our particular world, and what's more I'm afraid they'll go on happening from time to time whatever the comrade minister says.' He smiled wryly. 'Show me the country which has an unblemished record of successes in the intelligence field.'

'Those are dangerous thoughts,' Erika Grossman said grimly. 'They reveal flabbiness and bourgeois doubts such as one does not expect to find in the head of one of our most important sections.'

'I hope one wouldn't find flabbiness or bourgeois doubts *anywhere* in our department,' he replied. 'I certainly should never be a party to shielding any such corrupting influence. And nor, I know, would you, Comrade Grossman,' he added dryly.

Each of them was aware that the minister was a blustering fool who had achieved office by brazen manipulation and political chicanery of an unexampled order. Each of them was further aware that Erika Grossman's own career in the department rested on the bolstering presence of her subordinate.

'This is no time for argument,' she said, looking like a large, sullen child. 'Tell me exactly what has happened.'

'There isn't much to tell. Simply that we have had to close our Dahlem operation for the time being. I am already working on a new plan which can be put into immediate effect and which should prove as fruitful in the long run as the one we have had to scrap.'

'And our link?'

'Seagull? Gone underground.'

'Wouldn't it be better to recall our bird?' she asked sardonically.

He shook his head. 'Not for the time being. Our links always have prepared hideaways. One doesn't want them dashing back at the first hint of trouble.'

'This is more than a hint. This *is* trouble.'

'All the more reason for Seagull to move to the prepared positions in the opponent's territory and not come scampering back.'

'I am wondering whether the situation calls for your personal intervention . . .' she said dreamily.

'You are suggesting that I should arrange a visit to Dahlem myself?'

'Exactly.'

He shook his head in frowning annoyance. 'If that is an order, of course, I go, but I do not advise it. It is not that I am afraid of the dangers, though they naturally exist, but it would not achieve anything. The general should not play the lance-corporal, if you understand my meaning.'

'Very clearly. You do not wish to go into West Berlin.'

'That is so,' he replied tartly, 'and I hope my record is sufficient proof of my judgment in matters of this kind.'

'It was the comrade minister who suggested it,' she said, watching his expression.

He sighed wearily. 'It will ruin my plan if I have to go.' Beads of sweat began to glisten on his forehead. 'Can't the comrade minister leave the details to us?' His tone was agitated.

'One plan has already been ruined,' Erika Grossman said nastily. 'But, of course, I'll tell the comrade minister that you don't wish to do as he suggests.'

Fröhlich licked his lips which had become suddenly very dry. 'Try to persuade him,' he said urgently. 'It's very important not to resort to panic measures at a time such as this.'

'I only hope that the comrade minister won't consider you to have fallen into a panic at the mention of his suggestion.' She felt she had now sufficiently redressed the balance of his earlier sly impudence and gave him a wintry smile.

'This English lawyer,' she went on in a friendlier tone, 'I gather from reports he has learnt nothing.'

Fröhlich sniggered. 'He is the hearty amateur whom the British so much admire. With them "professional" is a dirty word, whether applied to sportsmen or to prostitutes.'

'Well, it seems he is wasting his time in Berlin,' she said, and went on scornfully, 'No wonder Crofton was jailed for twenty years if he had such a fool to defend his interests. Why didn't they give him a lawyer from the party?'

'In England that would have made it worse for him.'

Erika Grossman clucked impatiently. 'And now you had better tell me the details of your new plan. I hope it's as good as you promise, since matters cannot drift on as they are. It's results we must have, Comrade. Results and without further delay, too! Let us not forget that we shall be judged by the speed of our results and let us therefore bend to the task with fresh determination.'

'Well spoken, Comrade Grossman. Now, this is what I propose. . . .'

12

THE only communication awaiting Ainsworth when he arrived back at the hotel was a letter from Aunt Virginia. He retired to his bedroom to read it.

Dear Martin (it ran),

I hope you're enjoying your stay in Berlin, and not finding it too dull in August. It's not a good month for visiting large cities, as most of the better people have moved out, and so much is closed down. Have you ever been in Paris in August? Not a Parisian within a hundred miles, and all the best restaurants shut. I've played bridge several times since you left and had some enjoyable games. Happily that dreadful friend of May Thatcher's is away, so one is spared the wringing ordeal of drawing her as a partner. Mrs. Carp's husband has failed his driving test again, and she has a nasty boil somewhere out of sight. I don't think the two events are connected, though both have lowered her morale. Allison has written suggesting that you should join us in Scotland if you've nothing better to do. I have replied that you've gone off to Berlin to be nostalgic. Is it true they're replanted the limes in Unter den Linden? Once a letter gets reduced to questions, it's a sure sign to bring it to a close. So, with all my love,

Aunt Virginia.

Ainsworth put down the letter and stretched out on the bed with his hands clasped beneath his head. It was an overcast, sultry afternoon and everywhere seemed very quiet. Only the occasional clatter of a train on the overhead railway disturbed the peace.

Aunt Virginia's letter, with its air of astringent sanity, had managed to underline the futility of his mission. What on earth had induced him to come on such a mad undertaking? He'd made a real fool of himself when he'd allowed Bowes to persuade him. If he'd stopped to think, he must have realised that the whole plan was foredoomed to failure. What chance did he ever have of insinuating himself into Elli's confidence, so as to be able to wheedle all her black secrets out of her?

But even in the midst of this self-denigration, another part of his brain flew to the defence of his amour propre. Unless they'd envisaged the possibility of success, they'd never have approached him. Moreover, he may have come nearer to success than he knew.

However all that might be, here he was lying on his bed at half-past two in the afternoon at the loosest end at which he had ever found himself. If his own convenience weren't involved, he'd lie there until Lander came and begged him to get up.

There was a knock on the door and it opened to reveal Fräulein Grimmer.

'Herr Ainsworth,' she said severely, 'there is a notice asking visitors not to lie on their beds fully dressed.'

'I've taken off my shoes.'

'But your clothes still soil the covers.'

'Is that all you've come to say?' he asked, giving a wriggle to soil them a bit more.

'You are wanted on the telephone. Mr. Lander wishes to speak to you.'

Ainsworth swivelled his body off the bed and stood up.

'If he has rung off by the time I get there, I'll do worse than soil the bloody bed,' he muttered at Fräulein Grimmer's retreating back.

But Lander was still on the line when he reached the telephone at the top of the stairs.

'I'm sorry I've proved so elusive,' he said, 'but all hell's broken loose and I've not been in the office since first thing.'

'I've got a lot to tell you—and to ask you. When can we meet?'

'Can you manage now?'

'Yes.'

'Good. Then take the U-Bahn to Reichskanzlerplatz and I'll be waiting outside in the car.'

The next moment he had rung off. Five minutes later Ainsworth left the hotel and twenty minutes later stepped out of the Reichskanzlerplatz underground station. He spotted Lander's car parked about fifty yards along the road. As he approached, Lander lent across and opened the passenger door for him. No sooner had he got in when the car, whose engine was already running, pulled away with feverish acceleration.

'We'll go and park in the Grunewald and talk there,' Lander said briefly.

Ainsworth noticed that he looked drawn and didn't appear to have shaved that day, though there was still about him the same air of anonymous detachment which Ainsworth reckoned was now probably as much a part of him as his skin.

They drove for about fifteen minutes, then Lander made a right turn down a side road, and after a quarter of a mile pulled on to a track which ran straight into the wood. When he finally stopped, they might have been in the middle of an African forest for the stillness around them.

'We shan't be disturbed here,' he said laconically, 'so fire away.'

'How much do you know of what's happened since last night?' Ainsworth asked. He wondered if this was a regular rendezvous of spies and whether a similar assignation was taking place in the next glade. It all became more cloak-and-dagger-like each day.

'I know Frau Seidler has disappeared.'

'She's gone to see a sick aunt in Hanover I was told,' Ainsworth said to show that he'd not been wasting his own time.

'She hasn't left Berlin.'

'How do you know?'

'She's still in the city,' he said, brushing the question aside.

'In which part?'

'That depends on what further use they think they can put her to.'

'So she may still be in West Berlin?'

'Quite possibly.'

'Do you know about Koeslin?'

'You tell me what you know about him.'

'He's dead. Murdered. His body was left lying on Elli's sitting-room floor. We found it there when we arrived back from the restaurant last night.'

Lander was silent for a full half-minute as he stared thoughtfully ahead of him. 'No,' he said at length. 'No, I didn't know he was dead.'

'Who was he, anyway?'

'Koeslin? He was an agent of the East German Government,' Lander said slowly.

'Then who killed him?'

'How do I know?' His tone bore a trace of irritation. 'The big trouble about this city is that spying is in a thoroughly anarchistic state. There are far too many factions and splinter groups and middle-men all swarming over the scene and getting in one another's way.' He made a grimace signifying distaste. 'It is possible that someone went to the house to kill Frau Seidler, found Koeslin there and murdered him instead.'

'You make murder sound a very casual affair.'

'In our business it is always deliberate and invariably pitiless, but never casual.'

Ainsworth let this go. It was obvious that Lander had misunderstood his meaning, but it was scarcely the moment for discussing the niceties of political murder.

'Surely if the murderer had intended to kill Elli, you would know something about it.'

'Why do you say that?' Lander asked sharply.

'Because presumably it would have been one of your own side.'

'Ah! But even so, not necessarily. It is unfortunately true that the right hand doesn't know everything the left hand undertakes.'

'Have you known about Koeslin for a long time?'

'Yes.'

'You might have told me so when I reported his presence in the Hilton Hotel to you. You gave no indication then that you knew him at all.'

'It wasn't politic to do so. You must be aware, Mr. Ainsworth, that in intelligence work one is told no more than is strictly necessary for carrying out one's particular job.' He fixed Ainsworth with cold, grey eyes. 'Tell me the rest of what happened when you took Frau Seidler out yesterday.'

When Ainsworth had finished retailing the events of the previous evening, Lander said with an unwonted degree of animation. 'That's very interesting! You're quite certain that you recognised this man whom you followed when he left the house.'

'As certain as one can be after all that time.'

'What was his name again? Here, write it down on this piece of paper.'

'Gustav von Sternmeier. He was an old left-wing friend of Elli's husband.'

'Von Sternmeier,' Lander repeated thoughtfully. 'Describe him as fully as you can, will you? Don't omit a single detail. This is most interesting and possibly very important.'

'About six feet tall, with a bit of a stoop. Long hair, thin on top and receding in front. Looks rather like a university professor and walks with a loping stride.'

'Age?'

'Early fifties.'

'Complexion?'

'Muddy. And face a bit lined and mournful, but he has—or rather used to have—a delightful smile. He probably still does have.'

'And this is the man whom Frau Seidler pretended to know nothing about?'

'Yes. She first of all said she couldn't place him, then later told me she hadn't seen him since the war and assumed he was now dead.'

'This is most interesting, and possibly very important,' he repeated, giving Ainsworth a small approving smile.

'Good. What's my own position now?'

'I'll speak to others and let you know.'

'Because I'd like to get away tomorrow or the day after.'

'I'll give you an answer within twenty-four hours.'

'It's the first time I've ever heard you mention "others",' Ainsworth remarked sardonically.

'I'm not a one-man band,' Lander replied in an obviously-nettled tone.

'Well, tell your "others" that since Elli has disappeared and there doesn't seem to be any further use for my services here, I'd like to be off.'

'I'm sure no one'll want you to remain a minute longer than necessary.'

'I imagined it was Elli's disappearance and Koeslin's death which had been giving you such a busy day,' Ainsworth observed artlessly as Lander put out a finger to press the self-starter.

'Only partly so.'

He should have known that Lander was not likely to respond to so transparent a ploy. But since he had been of such potential help he didn't see why he should bottle up all the questions he was eager to ask.

'Do you think that von Sternmeier may be Elli's contact with East Berlin? Is that why you are so interested in him?'

'He is interesting,' Lander replied primly, 'because we did not know of his connection with Frau Seidler. From what you say, he must be in close contact with her and if he has known her all those years, well . . . there is something to be followed up and checked on.' He cast Ainsworth another of his tentative smiles. 'We may yet be able to endorse the papers "success of a mission".'

They drove in silence for a time. Then Lander said, 'Do you mind if I drop you at the next S-Bahn Station. You'll be able to get a train to the zoo. They run every few minutes.'

'No, that's all right. Shall I be able to reach you at the office if I want to get in touch?'

'I'm not sure when I'll be back. Better leave me to 'phone you.'

'Provided you do.'

'Naturally, I shall. After all, you're my charge,' he added with a wry grin.

'And don't forget I want to leave Berlin as soon as possible,' Ainsworth said as he got out of the car, 'mission successful or unsuccessful.'

Lander made no reply other than a vacant nod. Then thrusting the car into gear he accelerated away, leaving Ainsworth to feel that he wasn't even a memory in the rear-view mirror. On the way back to the hotel he did a considerable amount of hard thinking, and underwent the full range of ambivalent emotions which he had been experiencing ever since he'd arrived in Berlin.

By the time he reached the hotel, Ainsworth, the active adventurer, was in command and he had made up his mind to pay one further final visit to number fourteen Karolinerstrasse.

He felt that unless he personally could find out the truth about Elli, the exact nature of what she'd been up to was likely to remain shrouded in the mists of security. Elli, who had come so vividly back into his life, couldn't be allowed to leave it again without his discovering what lay behind her defection.

Thus resolved he laid his plans for the evening.

13

MARTIN AINSWORTH had not dined in the hotel since the first evening, but decided that he'd do so on this particular one. His decision was not made in any expectation of culinary delight, but because he felt the need to remain within the seclusion of the hotel until it was time to set out for Dahlem.

He entered the dining-room sharp on the bidden hour and nodded greetings at two of his fellow guests who had managed to beat him to it. One, he had learnt, was a civil servant in the Berlin City government; the other, an elderly woman, was reputed to be a general's widow. Apart from two half-hour walks a day, which she took regularly at half-past eleven and a quarter-past four, she spent her whole time playing patience in the gloomy lounge next door to the dining-room. She was punctilious in her exchange of formal greetings but was not otherwise known to speak. The civil servant always read a newspaper with his breakfast and dinner (he didn't come back for lunch) and ambushed Ainsworth with a brisk 'Guten Abend' from behind the evening paper which hid him from view.

The waitress brought him a plate of soup which she spooned out of a vast tureen on the serving table.

'What sort of soup is this?' he enquired genially as she put it before him. 'A Doppelkraftbrühe?'

'Es ist eine Schildkrötensuppe,' she remarked tolerantly, as though only an idiot could mistake a Schildkrötensuppe, for a Doppelkraftbrühe. To Ainsworth's eyes the only difference between them was that this evening's had half a dozen small pieces of pasta floating uncertainly at the bottom of the plate, and they could well have got there by accident.

The soup was followed by a thick slice of tasty meat which he eventually identified as venison. With it was served one very pale boiled potato and some beans. The sweet consisted of a rather good cherry flan, covered with a mound of artificial cream which he scraped off.

He was just finishing his coffee when Fräulein Grimmer came into the dining-room. She paused at various tables rather like an orderly officer making his rounds, save that in the present instance he doubted whether any of his fellow guests would ever muster enough courage actually to make a complaint.

'Guten Abend, Herr Ainsworth,' she said primly, when she reached his table. 'Might I enquire whether you will be going out after dinner?'

'Yes, I shall be.'

'Will you be late?'

'Very probably.'

'After midnight?'

'Perhaps.'

'In that event, I will give you a key.'

'All right.'

'But I must ask you not to lose it and to return it to me personally in the morning.'

'That's a pity.' She looked politely puzzled. 'I mean about not losing the key. Normally I always make a point of doing so.'

He had the satisfaction of watching her fold her lips in frosty disapproval before she moved away to the next table. He wondered how much longer their cold warfare could continue without a real eruption. Fortunately he had every intention of leaving Berlin within the next forty-eight hours.

After dinner he returned to his room and lay down on his bed to think. He realised that the course of action he was set on was almost certainly imprudent, might prove futile and at worst could land him in considerable difficulties. On the other hand, it was *their* fault. They had aroused his interest in Elli and it was this interest which would now only be satisfied by some personal investigation. The actual dangers, whatever they might be, didn't worry him. He had sufficient faith in his own star and didn't seriously believe that any would materialise. As to difficulties in which his action might land him, well, he reckoned he would be able to talk his way out, if the worst came to the worst. The inhibitions which would have deterred him in London were removed in a foreign city, as is invariably the case. What would seem unthinkable at home merely had the flavour of adventure when contemplated abroad. Chambers, membership of his club, even Aunt Virginia all lost their restraining influence at this distance.

At ten o'clock he collected a key from Fräulein Grimmer and left the hotel. The Kurfürstendamm was crowded with strolling people. The cafés were all full, and everywhere the neon shone

113

with enticing brightness. It was difficult to realise that little over a mile away the wall squirmed its sinister path across the city. There at this moment few people would be about, and instead of coloured neon, harsh light would be illuminating the killing ground on the wall's far side. Beyond its range only shadows flickered across the surrounding acres of desolate rubble.

He passed the offices of Kudos City Tours. Two coaches were parked outside waiting to take visitors on a round of Berlin night clubs. He recognised one of the drivers as the man who had driven him on the city tour the day after his arrival. He had since learnt that the drivers of these sightseeing coaches were amongst the numbered few who had passes permitting them to enter East Berlin. Presumably they were considered to be silent and harmless, whereas the guides with their virulent anti-East views had of necessity to be excluded from Herr Ulbricht's portion of the city.

A tired-looking man with a bald head thrust a leaflet at him as he passed.

'Night club tour, sir?' he said with mechanical enthusiasm. 'Very interesting. You go to four different clubs. There is champagne and much interesting things to see.'

'No, thanks.'

From all accounts Berlin's night life still catered for the connoisseurs of the bizarre, if not as opulently as Hamburg's.

He walked on past the Kaiser Wilhelm Memorial Church which shone a grotto-like blue.

Leaving the bright lights of the Kurfürstendamm behind him, he made his way to Wittenbergplatz from where he could take the U-Bahn direct to Dahlem. As the short yellow train came bursting out of the tunnel and he got in, he reflected on how much of his time in Berlin seemed to have been spent travelling on underground trains. However, it was a considerably more tolerable method of getting about than in most other cities. It was clean and never too crowded—at least not at the hours he travelled.

On this occasion he decided to travel on to Thielplatz, which was one station beyond Dahlem Dorf. It meant no longer walk to Elli's house which was near enough equidistant from the two stations, but it seemed a sensible precaution to break the normal routine of his approach.

Karolinerstrasse had its usual nocturnal air of graveyard

silence as he walked with conscious stealth along the pavement. A light shone from the Kramers' bedroom window and he hoped they weren't sitting up waiting to raise the alarm at the first untoward sound. Happily, the nightingale was providing another full-throated serenade which was calculated to drown any noise less than the discharge of a cannon.

The house next door to Elli's was again in darkness and Ainsworth decided to climb over into her garden at the same spot he'd done so the previous evening. He once more carried an armful of logs with him and set them up as before. There was no sign that anyone had been over that part of the garden in the intervening period and in fact it now seemed likely that the house was shut up and the occupants away.

This time he made a rather more delicate landing in Elli's garden, and avoided sinking in compost up to his shins. Standing on the edge of the shrubs he strained his gaze in the direction of the house. Curtains were half-drawn, but there were no lights on inside and it seemed certain that no one was at home. He suddenly grinned in the darkness as he wondered what all the burglars whom he had defended and prosecuted in his time would say if they could see him now, contemplating his own introduction to their ranks.

Moving round the perimeter of the small side lawn until he reached the rear of the house, he then flitted across the few open yards which separated him from the back entrance. It was the kitchen window rather than the door which attracted his interest. Before giving it a close examination, however, he slipped on a pair of grey cotton gloves which he had bought that afternoon. The window opened outwards and appeared to be secured by a single catch in the centre of one side.

Pursing his lips with determined decision, he extracted a screwdriver from his pocket (another purchase of the afternoon) and inserted it between the edge of the window and the jamb. Then exerting considerable leverage he tried to force the window open. At first nothing happened and he brought the screwdriver lower down the frame. This time there was an ugly sound of splintering and a piece of wood struck him smartly in the face. The window itself, however, remained firmly secured. He retreated quickly into the shadow of the shrubs and waited. If there was anyone in the house they must certainly have heard the noise. But it remained without sign of life and the nightingale's song continued uninterrupted. To Ainsworth it sounded more than ever like an opera singer past her best, though he was grateful at this moment for the bird's unquenchable stamina.

He once more approached the defiant window and thrust the screwdriver in near the catch and levered. He could feel it yielding slightly to the pressure, though he was still doubtful which would give way first, the window, the screwdriver or himself. He paused and massaged the palm of his hand. Now for a third and final trial of strength. There was a sudden noise of ripping wood and the window flew back on its hinges, banged against the wall and the glass splintered over the ground.

Shocked by what to his ears had sounded like the release of half the devils in hell, Ainsworth retreated hastily into the shrubs and waited a full minute before anxiously peering out. The nightingale had certainly stopped singing, but otherwise everything seemed as before. Nevertheless, he decided to creep round to the front of the house under cover of the bushes and make sure that all was still quiet in the street outside.

The Kramers' bedroom light was out and their house in darkness. It remained so during the five minutes he stood there with eyes and ears alert. He realised with relief that the sound must have been largely masked by the house itself and had possibly not been as ear-splitting as he'd feared.

He returned to the rear of the house and climbed in. The first room he made for was the small study where the desk and telephone were. The desk was locked but opening it proved an easier task than had the kitchen window. Though he had pulled the curtains across, he didn't risk switching on the light and used the torch which had been his third purchase of the afternoon.

It required only a glance to see that the desk had been cleared of almost all its contents and his only hope was that something had been overlooked in the haste of Elli's departure. His fingers dived eagerly into the backs of drawers and pigeonholes. In one of them he found a folded newspaper cutting. He opened it out to discover that it came from an English newspaper—probably the *Telegraph*—and was an extract of his closing speech to the jury in the Crofton case. So Elli had clearly known a great deal more about that than she had let on. This didn't surprise him, though it was interesting to receive confirmation of the fact.

Having gathered the desk's remaining contents in front of

him, he now began to sort through the various items. He had almost completed the task and was despairing of finding anything of further interest when he came upon a fragment of paper which he recalled having fetched out from the back of a pigeonhole where it had partially slipped down a crack.

It was crumpled and dirty round the edges, and on it in fading pencil was an address, 'Veldstrasse 16'. Ainsworth fished from his pocket the street plan which he had been carrying about since his arrival. A minute later he was studying the piece of paper with a deeply thoughtful expression, for he'd discovered that Veldstrasse was in East Berlin.

Although following his first visit he had felt certain that the desk concealed a radio transmitter in one of its drawers, he could find no trace of anything which might be remotely connected with such a piece of equipment and concluded that he must have been mistaken.

He moved next into the sitting-room, carefully drew the curtains across, and by the light of his torch continued his quest for clues to Elli's activities. As the beam traversed the room, it fell on the framed photograph of himself. Evidently she hadn't felt the need to take it with her as a cherished memento. He went over and picked it up from the table. Had he really looked like that? He remembered assuming what he'd considered to be a suitable expression of maturity behind which he hoped the perceptive would be able to note a blend of strength and dashing spirits. The result was a photograph of a young man struggling to fight back an attack of nausea.

He took it from its frame and examined the back in the wild hope that it might reveal some secret message. All he found was a piece of sententious verse of which he now recalled with shame being the author. Like most young men of every generation he had passed through that idyllic phase.

Leaving the sitting-room he went upstairs where an examination of Elli's bedroom indicated the hurry in which she had departed. Drawers and cupboard doors were still open and their remaining contents heaped untidily together. But he found nothing of any significance, and after a cursory glance in the bathroom and the sparsely furnished spare bedroom, he returned downstairs again.

As might have been expected, all record of her activities had been effaced. Only the piece of paper with the East Berlin

117

address bore any interest and that might prove to be short-lived, though it was definitely worth further investigation. He re-entered the small study and gave the desk his attention once more. It was just possible that a closer scrutiny of its contents might yield something further.

As he began to sift through the various items, consisting mainly of receipts, advertising leaflets and some concert programmes, and was riffling the pages of one of the programmes, some pencilled writing suddenly caught his eye. He turned back to the page and there found scrawled in the margin in Elli's hand the name *Koeslin*. Beneath was written, *coming across shortly—will enrol as student.*

He noticed that 'Koeslin' appeared in quote marks, which seemed to indicate that it wasn't his true name. Why else should it so appear? And if it wasn't his real name, who was he and why did he require a false identity? These questions chased through his mind as he continued staring with a frown at the cryptic message he held in his hand. *Coming across shortly.* The significant word in that trio was undoubtedly *across*, and in divided Berlin it could have only one meaning.

Somebody was telling Elli to expect a new student at her school who would shortly enrol in the name of Koeslin and that he was coming from East Berlin. Well, Koeslin *had* arrived and enrolled, and was now dead.

He gave a small grunt of satisfaction as further pieces of the puzzle fell into place. She must have just returned from a concert when the telephone had rung and she had written the message down on the nearest bit of paper which happened to be the programme she was holding in her hand. It accounted, too, for the scrawled appearance of the writing and its drunken slant.

The originator of the message must be her contact in East Berlin, and it looked as though Koeslin had come over to form a fresh link in the chain.

Ainsworth felt pleased with his deduction, though it did nothing to solve the mystery of Koeslin's death. Pocketing his two precious clues, he moved towards the door. There didn't seem to be anything further to be learnt in the house, and though his burglarious visit had failed to supply an answer to the most burning of his questions, he reckoned that it had not been without purpose.

He climbed back out through the kitchen window and then wedged it shut with a piece of wood so that it wouldn't swing open with the first puff of wind. In less than a couple of minutes he was over the fence and in the next-door garden. This time he didn't bother to collect the logs and return them to their pile outside the garage. Since it was going to be obvious how he had got into Elli's house, it hardly mattered that anyone should also find out how he'd gained entry into her garden.

He paused by the front gate before stepping out into the street, but everywhere was quiet and there wasn't even the sound of a distant car. He glanced in the direction of the Kramers' house and congratulated himself on not having disturbed their rest.

A car turned into Karolinerstrasse as he reached the end and he instinctively flattened himself against a tree. It stopped, as far as he could judge, outside the house beyond Elli's. The lights were extinguished and he heard a door slam. After that he waited no longer, but hurried in the direction of the underground station.

It was with considerable relief that he found he hadn't missed the last train. As he journeyed back into the centre of the city he experienced an almost intolerable weariness. It was as though he'd been playing five sets of singles in a needle match, and he decided to call in at one of the late-shutting cafés on the Kurfürstendamm and have a nightcap.

By the time he was on his second large Scotch, he felt considerably revived and distinctly pleased with himself. Looking back on the events of the evening he reflected on all the things which might have gone wrong but hadn't. Though he'd been prepared to talk himself out of any trouble, he now realised that in the event of his having been caught in the house this might have been easier contemplated than achieved. It could have been particularly awkward if Captain Kramer had sounded the alarm and he had found himself surrounded by civilian and military police of two nations. None of this had happened, however, and he was safely back midst the bright, comforting lights of the Kurfürstendamm.

He paid for his drinks and strolled off in the direction of the hotel. As he felt in his pocket he thought for one awful moment that he had lost the key Fräulein Grimmer had given him, only to discover that it had fallen through a hole in the lining of his jacket pocket. He let out a sigh of relief.

Turning into the street in which the hotel was located, he noticed a car parked at the opposite kerb. Almost before he had realised what was happening, two men had got out and were converging on him. They closed in on either side. The larger one said in excellent English: 'Come with us, Mr. Ainsworth, we want to talk to you.'

His tone, though quiet, brooked no refusal, and Ainsworth found himself being firmly escorted across the road to the car. Everything happened so swiftly that it was only after he'd been bundled inside and was being driven off at high speed that he had time to feel really frightened.

14

HANS FRÖHLICH hummed nervously to himself as he moved about the small living-room of his flat. He had always known that this moment would come, but he wished that it could have been at his own choosing instead of being forced upon him by events beyond his control. But that was where part of the rub lay, for they shouldn't have moved beyond his control in the way they had. He paused in the act of winding up his travelling clock to reflect on this. He didn't blame Erika Grossman even though none of this might have happened if she had stood up to the impatient bluster of the minister. No, the real culprits were Koeslin, their own man, and the enquiring British lawyer who had arrived suddenly out of Elli's past and conducted himself with all the finesse of a moth round a naked light.

He straightened an ornament and sat down, only to spring up again a second later and resume his restless prowl. In another half-hour it would be time to go. The prospect of these sorties into West Berlin always sent a shiver of apprehension down his spine. There was always danger involved, and he was getting too old for field work, anyway. He recalled how insistent Erika Grossman had been that he should undertake the assignment himself. Too insistent, he had felt at the time, and had wondered what treacherous thoughts lay behind her plump, waxen face. But he still didn't bear her any ill-will. With Erika as with every good comrade, personal relationships were subordinate to the interests of the party.

And tonight there would be additional dangers. Tonight events would move to their climax and nothing he could do now would stem their course. Sooner or later it had been bound to happen, and perhaps now was, after all, better than later.

Only two things remained to be done and then he must be on his way. He went across to the desk in the corner of the room and taking a plain sheet of paper wrote on it:

'Going into the country for a few days. H.'

He placed it in an envelope which he addressed to Herr Wilhelm Schmidt in the East Berlin suburb of Treptow. Next

121

he went into his bedroom and changed his clothes. When he emerged he was wearing the uniform of a postal official.

Then with one final fond look round his flat he picked up his satchel and the letter and let himself out.

It was after midnight and Veldstrasse was deserted.

Martin Ainsworth clenched his fists until he thought the bones must crack. But better the bones of his hand than his nerve at this critical moment. He cast a surreptitious glance at his captors and saw nothing to reassure him. They were grim-faced and tough-looking. The one who was sitting beside him in the rear of the car wore the uncompromising air of a strong-arm security guard, taciturn and as flexible as a concrete block. The driver was a bit younger but obviously came out of the same mould.

Ainsworth reckoned he had a little less than ten minutes before they reached the wall. Clearly they wouldn't attempt to cross at Checkpoint Charlie with its American, French and British military police on round-the-clock duty. No, they'd almost certainly aim for one of the quieter crossing points which was open only to Germans, and which they would hope to pass through without hindrance on the west side. Nevertheless, they'd have to slow down in order to manoeuvre the car through the narrow slit and that would be his opportunity to raise the alarm, or better still make his escape.

He glanced at the door handle to his left and went through the motions of escape in his mind. Of course it would all depend on the man at his side not wishing to shoot him down. If the fellow wasn't under any inhibitions about this, then that would be the end of him, but it was a risk he must take. He hoped he wasn't being optimistic in believing that the man would be reluctant to shoot.

It was time to try to make out which route they were taking. He was thankful that he knew his Berlin well enough to recognise landmarks in most quarters of the city.

For a second or two he was puzzled as he focused his attention outside. It seemed that they were heading in the direction of Charlottenburg, and away from the wall. Then suddenly it dawned on him what was happening. They had foreseen the problem of smuggling him from West to East Berlin and instead were going to exit into East Germany. In a few minutes they would be on the autobahn speeding south-westwards in the direction of Potsdam, which lay on the far side of the wire perimeter. He felt momentarily stunned by the impact of his inference and mocked by his earlier hopes. Then he realised that it, at least, gave him more time in the western sector of the city and that meant greater opportunity to effect his escape. But did it? How did one escape from a car speeding down an autobahn at sixty miles an hour? His only chance would be if it was halted by traffic lights before they reached the autobahn.

They were now heading down a straight broad highway. There was little traffic about at this hour of the night and the driver was maintaining a steady forty. Ainsworth peered ahead with the desperation of a ship-wrecked sailor searching the horizon for a friendly puff of smoke.

Yes, there were some lights coming up. What's more they were red. He felt the driver ease his foot off the accelerator and then push it hard down again as they switched to green and shone tauntingly in his despairing eyes as the car sped over the cross-roads. Two hundred yards ahead was another set of lights, already at green. If mesmerism could succeed in such circumstances they must remain so until the car was about thirty yards short and then change. He could tell that the driver was in two minds whether to slow down now, or to accelerate in the hope of beating them. Surely they must change any second now. Fifty, forty, thirty yards and still green. Twenty and with the car gaining speed, they were suddenly red. It was clear the driver was going to ignore them, when from their right an enormous pantechnicon and trailer pulled straight across their path. There was a screech of tyres and it seemed to Ainsworth that the windscreen and dashboard were both flying back in his face. The man beside him let out a grunt as his head struck the driver's shoulder. A second later, Martin Ainsworth was out of the car and running harder than he ever had before. As he reached the further pavement, he threw a look over his shoulder and saw that both men were starting after him.

He sprinted on, only to realise at once, and then too late, that it would have been wiser to have kept to the main road. Its lights and the chances of meeting a friendly policeman would have outweighed the value of the covering darkness into which he was now recklessly plunging. There were street lights but they were well-spaced and surrounded by pools of deep shadow.

On either side were houses and the occasional small block of flats.

Ainsworth paused for a second to regain his breath and listen. He could hear the sound of running feet in the distance and realised with a small crumb of satisfaction that he had drawn away from his pursuers. On the other hand he had little doubt that their staying power would be greater than his.

Everything was suddenly quiet and he realised that they had also halted to take stock of the situation. They must be wondering whether he had taken refuge in one of the gardens. Should they begin to search as they went, or continue full tilt along the road in the hope of picking up the trail? Well, that was their problem and he could only trust that their decision would confound them. Meanwhile he couldn't afford to remain standing in the shadows any longer.

Moving forward more slowly but with greater stealth, he put another two hundred yards between himself and his hunters. When he stopped again it was to find himself outside a new block of flats, set back from the street and built round three sides of a square. Hesitating only a second, he ran across to one of the lighted entrances and tried the door through the glass panels of which he could see an inviting lobby. It was carpeted, and a deep sofa and two armchairs stood in the glow of a slender standard lamp. Its welcoming air stretched out towards him, but the door was locked. He had a sudden panicking urge to press his hand against all eight of the doorbells in the panel at his side—and keep it there until every occupant was alive to his plight.

But even while he was deciding what to do next, he heard footsteps approaching down the street. They had split and each was covering one side. Quickly he nipped round the edge of the building and ran until he reached the cover of the far end. There was an emergency exit and inside a flight of stone steps. The door opened with an appalling creak and repeated the sound as he pulled it gingerly to behind him. He took the stairs two at a time. On each floor a door led through to the main landings, but these were secured on the inside.

He reached the top of the stairs, passed through a door which wasn't locked and found himself on the flat roof of the building. Dodging round the various excrescences he tip-toed forward to the front edge and, from a kneeling position, peered cautiously over. His two pursuers were standing beneath a street lamp directly opposite the flats, apparently in earnest consultation. From time to time the senior one glanced sharply about him, and once he stared straight up at the roof where Ainsworth was. Luckily it was not a night for silhouettes, and Ainsworth doubted whether he could be spotted unless he stood upright and waved his arms about.

They must surely move away soon, and then, after giving them a reasonable time, he would make good his own escape. To his surprise and apprehension he saw someone cross the street and go up to the two men. In the same moment he realised the person must have come from the flats, he was aware of his two pursuers examining the building with undisguised interest. A few seconds later, escorted by the newcomer, they crossed the road and disappeared from his view in the lee of the block.

It seemed all too obvious that one of the occupants of the flats had either seen or heard him, and had now put his kidnappers back on to his track. As he looked helplessly about him he was torn by despair and fright and an upsurge of angry determination. Once they reached the roof, and in could be only a matter of minutes before they did so, he was bound to be spotted. It was devoid of hiding-places, and the various shapes which sprouted from its flat surface would afford him no more security than a lone palm tree in a desert.

Creeping to the edge of the roof, he peered right over. Although the building was only a three-storey one, it was a sheer drop to the ground, and with the odds of landing on a concrete path for anyone who cared to chance it. He moved silently over to the door, opened it a crack and listened. As he did so he heard the tell-tale creak of the door at the bottom and knew he hadn't long to wait now.

There was just one hope, namely to barricade himself in on the roof. The door opened inwards on to the stairs and had a looped handle on the outside. He had noticed one or two lengths of tubular scaffolding lying about, and if he inserted one of these through the handle, and it was wider than the door itself, then he would have effectively barred their entry.

In his excitement, he didn't pause to think further. For all his feverish activity during the next minute, he might have been proposing to live out the remainder of his life on the roof.

He got the piece of metal into place only seconds before he

heard footsteps on the far side of the door. He retired behind a water tank to observe events. Almost immediately the door was given a vigorous rattling, but he saw with a sense of rising triumph that it held fast. It was going to require more than that to prise it open.

But what now? He looked at his watch and saw that it was nearly one o'clock. It felt more like four a.m. three days later. Surely his would-be captors wouldn't hang about too long. They could hardly expect to maintain their bluff for ever. It was one thing to fool a single person in the middle of the night, quite another to take on the whole of West Berlin in broad daylight. If he could hold out for five or six hours, he must be saved.

He wondered what was happening on the other side of the door. Everything was eerily quiet. For ten long minutes it remained so, then there was a shattering noise which made him almost fall out of his skin.

Somebody was hacking at the door with an axe. Before his stunned gaze a hand came through the gash and slid the bar free. The door was pulled open and a man wearing West Berlin police uniform came out on to the roof, revolver in hand. Behind him, Ainsworth could see his two pursuers, and to their rear a group of eagerly curious faces.

'Wer ist da?' the police officer called out harshly.

Ainsworth stepped out from behind the cover of the water tank. As he did so, the officer raised his revolver and pointed it directly at his stomach. Then flanked by the other two, he approached the spot where Ainsworth stood cemented to the ground.

'Ist dies der Mann?' he asked the senior.

'Ja, das ist Ainsworth.'

Ignoring his two pursuers but urgently fixing the attention of the officer, Ainsworth said in faltering German, 'These two men are trying to kidnap me and take me into the East Zone. I demand you telephone the British Consul-General.'

Turning to one of the men, the officer grimaced and said, 'Ist er verrückt?'

'No, I'm not mad,' Ainsworth broke in. 'I'm telling you the truth. They're East German agents. If you let them take me, there'll be the biggest diplomatic rumpus the city's ever known.'

The larger of his two pursuers now stepped forward.

'There'll be a far larger rumpus if you don't accompany us

without further fuss,' he said in a low menacing tone. 'I don't know who you think we are, but we happen to be from British Military Headquarters. You've caused enough trouble for one night and if you won't come peaceably, I'll turn you over to this officer. He's got enough to keep you locked up for a while.'

'How do I know you're British?' Ainsworth asked stupidly.

The man produced a pass bearing the name of Harmshaw, and held it out at arm's length. 'Does that satisfy you?'

'Then why were you trying to kidnap me?'

'We want to interrogate, not kidnap you.'

'What right have you to interrogate me?' Ainsworth demanded, stung by the other's cutting tone.

'We reserve the right to interrogate anyone who comes blundering under our noses.'

'Are you officers of the Security Service?'

'The description fits,' the man replied laconically.

'And if I do come with you, where are we going?'

'To our headquarters.'

'Where's that?'

'In Charlottenburg. Not far from here.'

'Are you the same lot as Lander?'

'That's enough questions for the time being. Are you coming with us or going off to a German cell?'

'I'll come with you,' Ainsworth said wearily.

'That's wise of you. It wouldn't make all that difference to us, mind you, but it's the right decision from your point of view.' He turned to the police officer and spoke to him in German. At the end the officer returned his revolver to its holster, saluted and walked back to the door where at least a dozen people stood in an expectant throng, mostly in night attire beneath their raincoats. He shoo-ed them back down the stairs, leaving Ainsworth and his two captors alone on the roof. Harmshaw now spoke to the driver. 'Better go and fetch the car, Dick. I'll wait here with our friend till you get back.'

Ainsworth felt no inclination to talk. He was too stunned and bewildered by the events of the night to express rational thought, but realised that he must try to re-assemble the splintered pieces of his mind before they arrived at their destination.

'O.K., we'll go down now,' Harmshaw said about ten minutes later.

The staircase was deserted, though Ainsworth was vaguely aware of curtains being discreetly pulled aside as they passed along the front of the building to the waiting car.

It took no more than five minutes to reach their destination, which was a small office block in a quiet street not far from the Olympic Stadium. As they entered, Ainsworth noticed the sign beside the door. It read: '

'ANGLO-GERMAN MONTHLY PUBLICATIONS LTD.'

Although it was half-past one, there were lights burning in several of the rooms. Harmshaw gave a thumbs-up sign to the door-keeper and led the way up a flight of stairs and along a corridor to the last room on the left. He knocked on the door and opened it.

'I've brought Mr. Ainsworth, sir,' he announced nonchalantly and stood to one side to let Ainsworth pass.

Sitting behind a neat desk was a man of about Ainsworth's own age. He wore spectacles and had a rather mild expression which was emphasised by a shock of unruly hair. This was mouse-coloured though flecked in places with grey.

'Come in, Mr. Ainsworth. If I'd known you were going to be so reluctant, I'd have come to persuade you myself.' He had risen as Ainsworth came in but now sat down again. 'Have a chair. We have a fair amount to go through together, but first of all I'd better introduce myself. My name's Noyce and I'm in charge of this particular outfit.'

'You work late hours for a publisher,' Ainsworth remarked sourly.

Noyce smiled politely. 'Surely we don't need to beat about that bush. Now for a start perhaps you'd tell me what brought you to Berlin.'

'I'd have thought you knew the answer to that. Or at least could know with a little trouble.'

'Why do you say that?'

'Because I came here at the request of one of your cloak-and-dagger sections.'

'One of mine?'

'One of someone's, the government's if you like, I don't know the intricacies of your organisation. Except this seems to be another prime example of the right hand not knowing what the left is up to.'

'That certainly does happen occasionally,' Noyce agreed in a puzzled tone, 'but . . .' Then looking up, he said flatly, 'But nothing! Who told you to make contact with Frau Seidler?'

Ainsworth didn't immediately reply but sat staring ahead of him. He felt tired, dirty and generally bitter at the course of events in the previous twenty-four hours. He was almost ready to throw in his hand and curse the lot of them as he did so. Why should he go on bothering any further? He'd run enough risks on their behalf, not merely to life and limb, but to reputation, career and self-esteem which were even more important. All he knew at the moment was that everything had lost its perspective. He had been abruptly cast into a world of distorting mirrors where reality assumed the shapes of a nightmare.

At length, with a heavy sigh, he said, 'Before I begin answering your questions, will you get in touch with Lander, Stephen Lander?'

He noticed Noyce flash a look at Harmshaw who was sitting somewhere behind him.

'Stephen Lander is missing at the moment,' Noyce said in a careful tone.

'What do you mean by missing?'

'Just that we are not able to get in touch with him.'

'Is he a member of your outfit?'

'As a matter of fact, he's not.'

'But you know him?'

'Oh, yes. Ours is a small world.'

'Then you probably know that he was my contact in Berlin?'

Though Noyce's expression didn't change, Ainsworth had a strong feeling that he had caused him something of a surprise.

'Who was your London contact?'

'Robert Bowes, he was concerned in the Crofton case. As you may know I defended Crofton at the Old Bailey.'

Noyce nodded. 'Have you had dealings with anyone apart from Bowes and Lander?'

'Only Green. He 'phoned me in the first place and asked if I'd see Bowes.'

For a second, Noyce looked nonplussed.

'How much did they tell you about Frau Seidler?'

'Just that she was a Communist spy and that it was my job to see if I could discover her links with East Berlin.'

'Did they tell you the nature of her activities?'

'Not really. Bowes said she was thought to have had some connection with Crofton. He told me they could pull her in at any time, but hoped that by giving her a bit of rope they could learn something more, in particular about her channel of communication with her Communist masters. I remember he used the worm for a simile. He said if Elli was arrested before they learnt more about the network of which she was part, it was like cutting off a worm's head. It simply grew another.'

'Most descriptive,' Noyce observed dryly. 'And how much have you found out?'

'It's not for me to assess. Anyway I've passed it all on to Lander.'

'Unfortunately we shan't be in touch with Lander for a day or two, so perhaps you could repeat your findings.'

'Does Veldstrasse 16 mean anything to you?'

'It's an address in East Berlin,' Noyce replied evenly.

'Do you know who lives there?'

'Do you?'

'No, though I could make a wild guess.'

'Who then?'

'A man named von Sternmeier.'

Ainsworth noticed a brightening of Noyce's eyes. 'Who's he?'

'An old friend of Elli's. A pre-war Socialist friend, shall I say?'

'And you believe he's Frau Seidler's contact in East Berlin?'

'He could be one of them. I suppose you know all about Koeslin?'

'The young man found dead at Frau Seidler's house you mean?'

'Yes.'

'What have you found out about him?'

'He also belonged to East Berlin.'

'So! Have you any theories as to who killed him?'

'Von Sternmeier could have.'

'What makes you say that?'

'I recognised him as he left Elli's house on the night of the murder.'

'Where were you?'

Tired though he was, Ainsworth's face broke into a satisfied smirk. 'Observing events from a hiding-place.'

'Have you told all this to Lander?'

'Yes. I presumed he'd reported it.'

'Oh, I'm sure he has, but his report doesn't happen to have reached me yet.'

'Have you any idea what's happened to Elli? I don't imagine she's really gone to visit a sick aunt in Hanover.'

'I agree, it's most improbable.'

'Has she escaped?'

Noyce appeared to ponder the question, as though it presented exceptional difficulties. At length he said, 'Yes, I think you could put it that way.'

There was a short silence before Ainsworth said in a faintly hostile tone, 'I still await your explanation of the outrageous means adopted to bring me here. Do you really kidnap people off the street in the middle of the night?'

'Oh, it has been known before,' Noyce replied urbanely. 'And after all, you've behaved pretty outrageously yourself.'

'I beg your pardon?'

'Running away and breaking into people's flats and generally creating a most unseemly disturbance.' He pointed a minatory finger at Ainsworth. 'However, the thing was that we wanted to see you urgently, and couldn't risk your declining a less compelling invitation.'

Ainsworth let out a derisive snort. 'I've told you nothing which you couldn't have found out from your own people.'

'I think,' Noyce said quietly, 'that the time has come when I should inform you that there is no one of the name of Stephen Lander in our service, nor is there anyone of the name of Robert Bowes. Charles Green certainly exists, and he won't be too pleased to learn how his name was used to launch you on your assignment.'

Ainsworth swallowed uncomfortably. It was a long time since anyone had spoken to him in such quietly scathing tones. If only he weren't so tired.

15

ELLI SEIDLER turned over in bed for the umpteenth time. It wasn't the mere fact of it being a strange bed which was keeping her from sleep (for once this was a minor factor) but the turmoil of recent events had sent her mind feathering like a runaway propeller. And at the end everything had moved so rapidly. One minute all was normal, the next disintegration had spread with the deadly erosion of flood water. It all dated back to Martin's arrival. How difficult it was to realise that that had been but four days before! She felt there'd never been a time when he hadn't been subjecting her to insidious pressure. And to think that but for a silly slip on his part she might have been taken in; that she would probably have accepted his innocent explanation of how and why he came to be in Berlin. She hoped *her* employers didn't perpetrate similar stupidities, because lives rested thereon. 'How did you get hold of my address?' she had asked him that first evening when he arrived on her doorstep. 'I looked you up in the telephone book,' he had replied casually. If he had thumbed through the directory, he certainly wouldn't have found an entry relating to Frau Seidler of Karolinerstrasse 14, since she wasn't listed.

His slip had not only told her he was lying, but had indicated that the purpose of his visit was anything but innocent, and this had shocked and stunned her more than she could have conceived. That Martin who had played the knight in armour when she had most needed one, who had offered her marriage and been ready to risk his career and possibly his freedom for her, should return into her life decked out in basest duplicity, left her bewildered and numbed.

She had, of course, immediately reported his visit to her superiors and had thereafter followed their instructions. But it had not been easy keeping up the pretence, and when he had made his final blatant appeal to her emotions, she had almost faltered.

Presumably men must be stronger than women in such situations. At any rate they must have greater detachment and firmer control over their emotions.

She put out a hand to switch on her bedside light. Then propping herself up on one elbow she sipped water from the glass she'd put beside her. It was after two o'clock and she realised that she was now unlikely to go to sleep until dawn was breaking. It was always so. With a sigh she turned off the light and lay back against the hot pillow, surrendering her mind again to the fevered thoughts which possessed it.

How could Martin have lent himself to such despicable purpose, to come and play on her emotions in such a callous fashion. Ruefully she had to admit that those who had sent him had guessed shrewdly at her Achilles heel. If anyone could have wormed himself into her confidence, it would have been Martin Ainsworth. To give herself credit, however, she doubted whether even he would have succeeded so far as her work was concerned, but the risk of dropping an unguarded word would have been that much the greater in his company.

How could one man have changed so much? This was the question which re-echoed round her mind without receiving the satisfaction of even a partial answer. When a man such as Martin Ainsworth could behave so out of character, life became that much less secure. Elli groaned aloud as she sought repose for her weary body.

What irony that Martin, who at one period had helped her to re-build her life, should now have sent it toppling. For Elli had no illusions about the future. The employers of spies didn't waste time on sentiment.

16

TRAINED though he was to thinking quickly on his feet in court, Martin Ainsworth found his mind reeling helplessly under the impact of Noyce's bombshell. And in any event, three o'clock in the morning was not the best hour for receiving news of that sort, particularly after a day of such unaccustomed activity as he had just experienced.

Noyce looked across at Harmshaw and said, 'You might go and see if you can rustle us up some coffee, Peter. We shall be here quite a while yet.' Then he turned his attention back to Ainsworth. 'I take it you're prepared to carry on?'

'Do I have any choice?' Ainsworth asked dully.

. 'I suppose if you pleaded extreme fatigue, we should have to break it off, but I'm sure it'll be much better from all our points of view to get everything straightened out now.'

'Straightened out! At the moment everything's about as straight as the coastline of Norway,' he observed bitterly.

'Yes, it must be confusing for you,' Noyce said with a note of irony, 'so let's make a start. First of all this man Bowes, did he tell you for whom he worked?'

'He said he was a member of the British Security Service.'

'And you took that on trust?'

'No, I've told you, your great white chief Green asked me to see him—or at any rate somebody who said he was Green. And as I'd been introduced to Green at court a few days before by the Attorney-General, I naturally agreed. Furthermore,' he went on energetically, 'I remember that I did ask Bowes for some sort of proof of his identity.

'Oh?' Noyce sounded surprised. 'And what was his reaction?'

'He produced his official pass.'

'Official pass!' Noyce said with increasing surprise. 'What did it look like?'

'All I remember was that it bore his photograph and was signed by an Under-Secretary of State. And of course it had the Foreign Office stamp.

'I see.' Noyce's tone was provokingly non-committal.

'Well, what sort of pass should he have produced?'

'Not that particular one. Did he tell you what section he worked with?'

'No.'

'Or where his office was?'

'No. It had a Victoria telephone number.'

'But the fact that he never gave you an address didn't arouse your suspicions?'

'If I may say so, you're all so obsessively mysterious for much of the time that one hesitates to ask too many questions. If you're not hiding behind a box number, then you're masquerading as soft-fruit exporters or Channel Tunnel developers or as monthly publishers.'

'Without accepting the indictment, we'll nevertheless let it pass,' Noyce said suavely. 'Did Bowes tell you what part he played in the Crofton case?'

'No, but he seemed to know a good deal about it.'

'I'm sure he did.'

'If he doesn't work for you, who are his masters?'

'Can't you guess?'

'The other side.'

Noyce gave a mirthless laugh. 'Yes, the other side.'

'But which in particular?'

'Does it matter, everything eventually finds its way into the common pool.'

'And who is Bowes?'

Noyce reached out for a folder and opened it. 'Robert Bowes, aged thirty-eight, married and divorced, regular soldier with service in Far East and Kenya, commissioned as a quartermaster and attained the rank of captain, but lost this when cashiered for misappropriation of army stores and subornation of perjury. That was in 1959 in Hong Kong. Known to have felt embittered because bigger fish than he escaped unpunished. Returned to this country. Held a number of different jobs for short periods. Was dismissed from the last for embezzlement. Fought a long and unsuccessful battle with the War Office over compensation in respect of a house in Hong Kong he was forced to get rid of at a loss when his service came to a premature end. In 1961 he became mysteriously affluent again and was seen about in restaurants and bars he hadn't been able to afford. He was also known to have paid several visits to an Iron Curtain Embassy.' He glanced up. 'Those seem to be the relevant details of his career.'

'There isn't much you don't know about him.'

'It's a ceaseless game.'

'And I suppose Lander is in the same outfit.'

'That's so. Lander had an English mother and a Czech father. He came to West Berlin from Prague via Leipzig and Munich two years ago. From time to time our paths have crossed professionally, but until now we have never regarded him as a very important cog.'

'If you know so much about this couple, I don't understand why you didn't get on to me much quicker.'

'There are several answers to that. In the first place there's all the difference between knowing of someone's general activities and keeping them under twenty-four hour, round-the-clock surveillance. We just don't have the resources for that. In the second place when we did learn of your presence in Berlin, it still took us a little time to dig into your past. A search of your bedroom didn't tell us very much. It required reference to London.'

'And what's your verdict now?' Ainsworth asked in a weary tone.

'That you've been taken for the biggest ride since the Trojan Horse rumbled into Troy,' Noyce replied crisply.

'You could scarcely have made that sound less flattering.'

'I'm not interested in flattering you, Mr. Ainsworth. As far as I'm concerned you've been an unmitigated nuisance ever since you arrived. Indeed, you've been worse than a nuisance, you've——' He broke off as the telephone on his desk gave a discreet buzz. Lifting the receiver, he listened for several seconds in frowning silence. Then: 'Here, now, do you mean? No, all right I'll come immediately.' He replaced the instrument and gave Ainsworth a hard, thoughtful stare which looked like the preface of a renewed castigation. Instead, however, he said abstractedly, 'The coffee's just coming.'

A minute later the door opened and Harmshaw came in carrying a tray with two mugs on it. 'I didn't bring you one, sir.'

Noyce nodded in Ainsworth's direction. 'Stay with our friend, Peter, until I come back.'

For a time they sat sipping their coffee in silence, Ainsworth, for his part, gratefully. He didn't know whether it was really as good as it tasted, or whether his state of bemused exhaustion would have made hot dish-water equally acceptable. He could only assume that it was its beneficial effect which caused him suddenly to explode.

'I've just about had enough! For all I know, you're the im-
posters. You certainly behave a good deal less plausibly than
either Bowes or Lander. Why should I sit in this phoney building any longer? If you want me you can come and call on me at
my hotel, but you won't find me there very much longer because
I shall fly home on the first available 'plane.'

Harmshaw looked at him mildly, as though he were fully
used to such outbursts. 'You'd better wait till Mr. Noyce comes
back,' he said. 'I don't think he'll be very long.'

'Why should I wait?'

'Because you need our good will to get you off the hook with
the German police. That's why!'

Realising that he was temporarily beaten, Ainsworth swivelled
round in his chair to present as much as possible of his back to
the man. At least he could avoid looking at him. It was a petty
reprisal, but at that hour of the morning the civilised mind is
not very self-examining.

It was three-quarters of an hour before Noyce came back, by
which time Ainsworth had sunk into a state of exhausted indifference.

'I don't think we need ask you to stay any longer,' Noyce said
without preliminary. 'I'll arrange for a car to take you back to
your hotel. I shall almost certainly want to see you again, and in
any event I must ask you not to leave Berlin until I give you
the word.'

Ainsworth rose stiffly to his feet. 'Let me say for my part that
I still expect to receive a rather fuller explanation of events
than you have so far given me.'

'In this business no one is told more than they need to know,'
Noyce replied in a terse tone, 'and I've given you as much information as was necessary to prove to you that Bowes and
Lander are not what they pretended to be.' He turned to Harmshaw. 'Show Mr. Ainsworth the way out and get him a car,
would you, Peter.'

They had just reached the bottom of the stairs when Ainsworth caught sight of someone disappearing into a room along
the corridor to the left. Numbed by fatigue as he was, it still
struck him as a curious place, and even more extraordinary
hour, to see a postman. He only saw the man's back view, and by
the time the scene had registered he had gone.

137

17

AINSWORTH was awakened the next morning by a heavy knocking on his bedroom door. He glanced at his watch and saw that it was nearly ten o'clock.

'Herein,' he called out in a muffled croak.

The door opened to reveal Fräulein Grimmer looking like a monument to disapproval.

'It is ten o'clock, Herr Ainsworth,' she announced, and then folded her lips to await his reaction.

'I'm afraid I overslept. I came in very late.'

'And that is another thing, where is the key I lent you?'

'In my pocket.'

'I want it.'

'Certainly. If you hand me my trousers . . .'

'Please give it to me as soon as you are dressed,' she broke in, at the same time moving a step back. 'The maid is waiting to clean the room. I must draw your attention, Herr Ainsworth, to the notice which asks guests to vacate the bedrooms by half-past nine. Otherwise the work of the whole staff is disrupted.'

Ainsworth was by now sufficiently awake and irked by the intrusion to respond, 'May I suggest, Fräulein Grimmer, that you would be better at running a reformatory than a hotel. I'm tired of your rules. It's worse than being in the army.'

'Reformatory? I do not understand,' she said coldly.

'A women's penitentiary then. You might even be able to add to your apparently exhaustive list of rules. Though I doubt it. And now if you don't mind . . .' As he spoke he kicked off the bedclothes and Fräulein Grimmer closed the door with an angry gesture.

While he shaved, he tried to muster his thoughts to the point of reaching a decision as to what to do. He still felt in a state of bewilderment at the abrupt turn of events and was inclined to think that the most dignified course would be to inform Noyce that he would remain in Berlin for another twenty-four hours and that hereafter nothing and no one would prevent him returning to London. Once he was home it would be easier to decide what further action he should take. In the first place everything which had happened would be seen in a clearer perspective, and in the second he would have had the advantage of discussing matters in confidence with one or two of his closer friends.

He had just finished dressing when there was a further knock on his door, and a voice called out in German, 'Telefon, Herr Ainsworth.'

By the time he had reached the extension at the top of the stairs, he had made up his mind what he was going to say to Noyce. To his astonishment, however, it was not Noyce or one of his minions who answered, but Elli.

'I have to talk to you, Martin,' she said with breathless urgency. 'Meet me at the Café Liszt on the Kurfürstendamm in half an hour's time. On the right-hand side as you enter there are some tables in alcoves. Go to one of those if you arrive there before me. Is that all right, Martin?'

'Yes, fine, Elli, but where are you talking from?'

'I will explain everything when I see you. Café Liszt in half an hour.'

The line went dead and he realised she had cleared. Though his mind was momentarily cast into further turmoil by her call, he experienced an unexpected buoyancy of spirit. Here was an unhoped-for opportunity of learning the truth—and possibly his last.

Ainsworth arrived at the Café Liszt a few minutes early. There were six alcove tables but Elli was not at any of them. Four were already occupied and he chose the more secluded of the two which were free. He sat down and told the waiter who came bustling up that he was waiting for a companion.

He spotted Elli while she was still outside on the pavement and watched her come through the revolving door. She had on a white mackintosh, the collar of which was turned up, and her hands were thrust deep into the pockets. For a second or two she glanced quickly around, then walked over to where he was sitting.

'Hello, Martin,' she said gravely, offering him a hand.

He ignored it and bent forward to kiss her on the cheek.

'Your call came as a surprise,' he remarked with a faintly quizzical smile. Then as the waiter returned he asked, 'What are you going to have?'

'A plain Cinzano with a slice of lemon.'

'And for me, a lager.'

'I laid awake all night,' she continued, when the waiter had departed, 'and this morning I decided that I had to see you.' She avoided looking at him while she spoke. 'That was why I 'phoned you. I realise that I shouldn't be seeing you but . . . but——' She turned her gaze full on him. 'But in view of the past, I couldn't let you leave without knowing the truth. Martin, why did you come to Berlin to spy on me? What had I done to earn your contempt that you should undertake this mission, that you should try to deceive me so cynically about the reason for your visit?' She turned her head away and he saw that her eyes were filled with tears. 'Though I hadn't seen you for twenty-five years, I'd always thought of you with deep affection. I cherished your memory as no other. After all, was it not you who had saved my sanity and who had proved to be the staunchest friend even at personal risk? And then suddenly, after all these years in which I had only these memories, you turn up in person on my doorstep and almost immediately I realise that you have not come as the old friend you pretend to be, but as an opponent who is determined to conquer my resistance.' She shook her head wearily. 'I could not believe that this was the same Martin I had known.' Suddenly she looked straight at him again. 'I still cannot believe it. That is why I had to see you.'

He was silent for a minute or two, aware only of the apparent intensity of her feeling. Then he said slowly, 'I don't quite know where we now stand, Elli. I do know enough to realise that not everything is as I imagined it to be, but that doesn't mean I'm in possession of the whole truth. I've been told bits and pieces, but so far as your activities are concerned, I'm relying mainly on intelligent guesswork.' He made a deprecating grimace. 'However, here goes. I assume that you work for one of the allied intelligence services, is that right?' She made no response and he went on, 'O.K., you don't have to answer that, but perhaps it explains things if I tell you that I came to Berlin in the full belief that you were working for the other side.'

She looked at him incredulously. 'The other side?' she echoed in a puzzled tone.

'Yes, for the East German Intelligence Service. I was told you were a vital agent in one of their networks.'

'And you believed it?'

'Why not? I hadn't seen you since before the war. You had Socialist leanings in those days, so why should you not now be leaning a bit further to the left? What was so improbable about it?'

'But me a Communist?' Her tone remained disbelieving.

'Many more implausible things have happened to people in twenty-five years than that.'

'But who told you this lie about me?'

'Ah!' Ainsworth observed with a theatrical sigh and proceeded to tell her about Bowes and Lander and the scheme of which he had become an innocent part.

When he had finished, she was silent for a long time, then she said with a slight catch in her voice, 'I'm so glad, Martin.'

'Glad?'

'That none of the things I was being forced to believe about you are true. You see, I was certain that you must be a Soviet agent. There seemed to be no other explanation for your behaviour. It upset me terribly, but what else could I do but inform headquarters of your visit?'

'Is that Noyce's lot?'

She nodded. 'And they told me to play along with you and to try to find out exactly what you were up to. Oh, Martin, it was terrible and I hated it so!'

'How did I originally give myself away?' he asked curiously.

'When you told me you had looked up my address in the telephone book. You see, it isn't listed.'

'Good grief! To think that Bowes slipped up on that!'

'And then you caught me with all those questions about Gustav. . . . Seeing you became like a nightmare. . . .'

'Tell me about Gustav,' he broke in eagerly.

She looked anxiously about her before replying, then shrugged. 'Perhaps it does not matter now that we are finished,' she said, lowering her voice. 'After the war Gustav was a member of the Communist Party, but it did not last long. He became disillusioned with their aims and policies and began to see them as menaces instead of as saviours, so he decided that he must now work against them as vigorously as he had previously striven for them. He'd always lived in East Berlin, you may remember. Anyway he disappeared for a time and when he reappeared it was as Hans Fröhlich, a senior official in one of the sections of the Ministry of State Security. As such he was able to pass a lot of very valuable information to the West. Indeed it was his tip-off which led to the arrest of Crofton in England.'

Ainsworth nodded his head thoughtfully as pieces of the puzzle began to fall into place.

'I can see now that he must have been the hoped-for goal of my little mission. It was his identity they hoped I would be able to provide a lead to.'

'I think they must have known for some time,' Elli went on, 'that information was being leaked at a high level on their side, and they were naturally anxious to put their finger on whoever it was.' She gave a little shiver. 'And if they had succeeded it would have meant execution. But Gustav was always very brave,' she added quietly. 'Thank God, he got out safely.'

'Yes?'

'He came through last night dressed as a postman.'

'So *he* was the postman I saw at Noyce's headquarters.'

'In view of his trusted position in the ministry he could always get in and out of West Berlin, but he had to be very careful, as his visits were recorded.'

'Was that when he used to pass you information?'

'No. That would have been much too dangerous. We didn't dare have any direct contact with each other. He only came to my house once and that was the night before last because of the emergency. Koeslin was one of his ministry's men, you see. His people knew that I operated this end of a line, and so they sent Koeslin over in the guise of a student to try to discover where it led. In the same way that you were sent, Martin. It shows how determined they were to find out where the leak occurred.'

'And Gustav tipped you off about him?' Ainsworth broke in, remembering the scribbled words on the concert programme.

'Yes. Then a few days ago Koeslin got in touch with Gustav and asked him to come across into West Berlin for an urgent meeting as he had discovered something. So Gustav did come and they met and Koeslin was rather mysterious at first and said he would take Gustav somewhere and show him just what he had found. You can imagine Gustav's alarm when Koeslin led him to my house and then produced a duplicate key to let them in. Inside the house, Koeslin suddenly produced a revolver, and said he strongly suspected Gustav of being a traitor, and that he was going to hold him there at gunpoint until I came back, and then break us down in a confrontation.' Elli looked suddenly drawn. 'I think Comrade Koeslin saw himself sitting on Chairman Ulbricht's right hand in perpetual sunshine. However, Gustav managed to distract his attention, and then as he struggled to get the revolver it went off and Koeslin was shot.'

Ainsworth had no inclination to comment, glib though the explanation of Koeslin's death sounded. 'Presumably that all happened not long before we returned to the house?' he observed.

'Yes, Gustav only just had time to hide in a cupboard upstairs before we came in.'

'Who removed the body after I'd gone?'

'Noyce's men.'

'Of course, I should have guessed.' He thought for a moment, then said, 'There are only two more things I want to know, Elli. First, who lives in Veldstrasse?'

She looked at him in surprise. 'That was Gustav's address in East Berlin. How do you know about it?'

He gave her a sly grin. 'Koeslin wasn't the only resourceful spy on 'our' side. And the other question is, what was your system of communication with Gustav?'

'I should not tell you that,' she replied, 'but I will do as a token of my gratitude that you are, after all, still the same Martin. And if you are the same Martin, there is no secret with which I wouldn't trust you.' He tried not to show his embarrassment at this highly-charged sentiment, and Elli went on, 'There were two people in the chain between Gustav and myself. One of them was a driver for one of the coach companies which runs tours into East Berlin. The other was an old man who had a souvenir stall near Treptower Park where the coaches used to wait while the tourists went off to look at the Soviet War Memorial in the Park. On the days when there was anything to pass, the driver would choose a quiet moment to go across to the stall, and while he was buying a lemonade the old man would pass the information. When he returned to West Berlin, he would telephone me and we would meet somewhere. It was a rule he must never come to my house and I always had to be very careful that I wasn't followed when I went to the rendezvous.' She was reflective for a second. 'I can remember the first evening you visited me, the driver telephoned. He was worried about something and wanted to come and see me and I had to remind him firmly of the instruction.'

'And what about the old man with the stall in Treptower Park, is he safe, too?'

'Gustav sent him a pre-arranged message before he came across last night. The old man will be all right.'

'It's funny to think,' Ainsworth said slowly, 'that I may have ridden in the coach driven by your courier the day I went on my tour of East Berlin. I certainly remember an old man with a barrow-load of souvenirs in the coach park the other side.'

'But all of this you will keep entirely to yourself, Martin, yes?'

'I promise you that, Elli. May I ask you one more question?'

'If you wish.'

'How did you get drawn into all this?'

'Gustav originally brought me into it. We were lovers for a few months at the end of the war.' She smiled sadly at her thoughts. 'We had always been good friends and we still are, but we were not successful lovers. The trouble was that Gustav was more in love with the passion of his ideals than he was with me. It would have been better if I had remained what I had always been to him, namely a sister. He didn't want a mistress, still less a wife.' She straightened her back against the partition behind her. 'Anyway, it was Gustav who introduced me to a certain British officer and together they persuaded me to work for them. But do you know what persuaded me most strongly, Martin?' He shook his head. 'You! I thought to myself, "Here is a chance for me to repay Martin's country for having sent me Martin when I was in trouble with the Nazis."'

'I'm afraid my shining armour has become a little tarnished since then,' he remarked with an embarrassed smile.

'To think,' she went on, as though he'd not spoken, 'that I might not have telephoned you this morning and might never have known what you have told me.'

'I'm sure friend Noyce would have been happy to have supplied you with all the details of my elaborate deception.' His mouth twisted as he spoke. 'I've been taken for about the biggest ride anyone has ever had. I'm as big a monument to man's gullibility as the wall is to his inhumanity.'

'You shouldn't talk like that, Martin. Anyone would have fallen victim to such wiles.'

'Well, I hope so,' he said reflectively.

'You will get over it, too.'

'I shall certainly manage to do that. My self-esteem is only dented, not fractured.'

'There! Already you can joke about it.'

'Moreover, I've left more of a mark on events than a good many professional spies,' he went on. 'It'll be quite a time before I'm forgotten in Berlin's top espionage circles. What do you think they'll call me, the unprofessional spy?'

For answer, Elli stretched out a hand and took his.

'What a pity that our first meeting in twenty-five years had to be like this!'

'That's a piece of British understatement, Elli. Anyway, what are you going to do now?'

'I don't know. There is always the school, but perhaps I shall sell it. I don't know; it is too soon to plan the future. One must wait for the dust of the past to settle.'

He gave her hand an affectionate squeeze. 'Well, remember that the invitation to visit London is still open. Or perhaps I should say that the previous one is cancelled and a completely new one is issued as from this moment.'

'You are very sweet, Martin. May I let you know?'

'Any time, but don't leave it another twenty-five years.'

They stepped from the café and walked a few yards down the street together.

'I shall take a bus here,' Elli said suddenly. She lifted her face up to be kissed. 'Goodbye, Martin.'

'Aufwiedersehen, Elli.'

Their parting was over before either had realised it.

18

AFTER he had got back to the hotel, Ainsworth spent some time in aimless contemplation. He was reminded of the feelings he had once experienced at his prep school when, for some reason he couldn't now remember, he had had to remain behind a day after all the other boys had gone home for the holidays. He recalled the sensation of existing in a melancholy vacuum, which was precisely how he now felt. The sense of aimlessness paralysed the mind and filled him with a despairing lethargy.

It was not until afternoon that he was able to shake it off sufficiently to telephone Noyce and inform him that he proposed to fly back to London the next morning. He realised afterwards that he had almost hoped Noyce would veto the plan but he didn't, which meant that he then had to rouse himself to further positive action in making the necessary travel arrangements.

Fräulein Grimmer greeted the news of his departure with obvious satisfaction and lost no time in presenting him with his account. He spent the evening packing, and retired to bed immediately after dinner, still in a state of mental daze.

The next morning after breakfast he paid his bill and ordered a taxi. Fräulein Grimmer stood by the entrance as he left as though to make sure he didn't attempt to purloin any of the hotel property on his way out. They shook hands formally and she wished him a good journey, though he couldn't help feeling that if she were that evening to read that his 'plane had crashed in flames her only reaction would be to fold her lips in the satisfied knowledge that this, at least was not in breach of the hotel rules.

At Tempelhof Airport Ainsworth checked in and then strolled over to the bookstall. It was while he was thumbing through a copy of *Der Spiegel* that he heard a voice behind him.

'Good morning, Mr. Ainsworth.'

He turned to find Noyce and Harmshaw watching him with faintly-amused smiles.

'Good morning.' He returned the greeting as coolly as he could.

'We thought we'd come along and see you off,' Noyce said.

'What about a drink? We've got nearly half an hour before your 'plane leaves.'

As he accompanied them to the bar, he realised it was perhaps not unreasonable that they should wish to make sure that he really did depart. He wondered if they had arranged a special reception for him at the other end.

When their drinks had been served, Noyce said amiably, 'I don't know what Frau Seidler told you when you met at the Café Liszt yesterday, but I'm sure you will realise that almost certainly everything she did say to you would be covered by the Official Secrets Act. I'm sure you won't discuss any of these recent events once you get home.'

The veiled warning was not lost on Ainsworth, nor the sanction which underlined it. After all, Noyce knew as well as he that any revelation must inevitably lead to the further disclosure of his own hapless part in the whole business, and this he would scarcely relish.

'What's going to happen to Elli Seidler now?' he asked.

Noyce pursed his lips. 'We shall have to see,' he replied in the unsatisfactory tone of a grown-up dealing with an importunate child. After a pause he went on, 'Her usefulness in the particular venture was probably coming to an end anyway, though your arrival on the scene certainly precipitated matters.'

'You mean that Fröhlich was about to be uncovered in any event?'

'Ah! So you know about Fröhlich?'

Ainsworth felt once more like a small boy caught out by the headmaster. 'I knew him before the war under his other name.'

'Of course,' Noyce replied smoothly. 'However, to answer your question, yes, it's always only a matter of time before the likes of Hans Fröhlich get tracked down. And then it's even more a matter of time, a race against it in fact, whether they can make good their escape or whether they are caught and liquidated.'

'Have you any idea what's happened to Lander?'

'At the moment, no. And I gather your friend Bowes has also disappeared.' He gave Ainsworth a sardonic smile. 'But never fear, they'll turn up again. Good confidence tricksters always do.' Before Ainsworth could make any reply, he cocked his ear and said, 'There's your flight being called. We'd better go.'

'And what about Fräulein Grimmer? Was she part of someone's set-up?'

Noyce shook his head as he led the way to the departure gate. 'She's the one person you've encountered here who really is nothing more than she seems.'

'It's quite enough, anyway!' Ainsworth remarked, gathering up his belongings and preparing to follow.

His last view of them was standing on the tarmac watching the 'plane as it taxied out to the runway.

If his due arrival at London Airport was the object of attention from Noyce's people, it was done so unobtrusively as not to be noticed. Half-an-hour later he was in a taxi on his way to the flat.

He had sent Aunt Virginia a cable the previous night, but had an idea that she might already have left on her round of visits. This, however, turned out not to be the case, and he had hardly inserted his key into the lock when he heard her call out his name.

It was something of an affront to find the hall looking precisely the same as it had been when he left. After all he had been through in the past week, nothing, he felt, had the right to look the same again.

'And how was Berlin?' Aunt Virginia asked, emerging from the drawing-room and accepting a kiss on her small, smooth cheek.

'Very interesting.'

'I'm glad my cable reached you in time.'

'But I never received any cable.'

'You must have or you wouldn't be here, Martin.'

'What do you mean?'

'I sent you a cable yesterday morning telling you of that man's appeal. I don't know why chambers couldn't have sent it themselves, but I said I would. Your clerk pretended he wasn't sure where you were.'

'What man's appeal?' Ainsworth asked, in an attempt to disentangle the threads of Aunt Virginia's explanation.

'Crofton. Don't say you've forgotten who he is while you've been away.'

'Crofton's appealing?'

Aunt Virginia sighed. 'It's flying, it always leaves one stupid for several hours afterwards. I was reading an article by a doctor the other day and he said——'

'I never received a cable from you,' he broke in firmly. 'I sent you one saying I'd be back this afternoon.'

'I know. In answer to mine. It's lucky I've been able to arrange for Mrs. Carp to come and look after you, because I go up to Scotland tomorrow. Or have you forgotten that, too?'

'I thought Mrs. Carp was going off on holiday as well.'

'She's cancelled it because her husband's hurt his leg at work. I don't think she was very keen on a holiday, anyway.'

'Did John 'phone you about Crofton appealing?'

'Yes. He was in a state until I was able to tell him you'd be back. It's being heard by a special vacation court, he said. Crofton had apparently appealed without reference to his solicitor, but he would like you to act for him again.' She gave an impatient shrug. 'Anyway, it was something to that effect. I shall certainly complain to the Post Office about the cable not arriving. One doesn't spend all that money to send important messages into the void.'

'Are you sure you addressed it right?'

'Of course I did.'

Somewhere between Aunt Virginia and Fräulein Grimmer a cable had gone astray, but Ainsworth felt no inclination to carry the investigation further.

'I'll ring chambers in a minute,' he said.

'And so you found Berlin interesting?' Aunt Virginia went on. 'I'm glad you did. I suppose there's not much sign of the city you knew before the war?'

'No, not much.'

'Did you look up any of your old . . . acquaintances?'

He shook his head. 'I wouldn't have known where to start finding them.'

'I wonder,' Aunt Virginia mused aloud, 'what happened to that girl who used to run the pension you stayed in.' Ainsworth remained silent. 'I've forgotten her name again.'

When Ainsworth did telephone his clerk, it was to learn that Crofton's appeal was due to be heard in six days' time. He attended chambers the next morning to read the grounds of appeal, which were simply that there was insufficient evidence to support the jury's verdict, and that the judge should not have left the case in their charge. He sighed and stared out of the window with an abstracted expression at the distant Thames. It was, of course, not the first time he had been asked to go into court and make bricks without straw.

The Gothic emptiness of the Law Courts echoed with his footsteps when six days later he made his way from the robing-room to the Lord Chief Justice's Court. It was like being in St. Pancras Station at two o'clock on Christmas morning, and it wasn't until he reached the court that any sign of life manifested itself.

Promptly at half-past ten three red-robed judges took their seats and Crofton was ushered into a small curtained enclave at one side of the court-room. He caught Ainsworth's eye and gave him a small nod of greeting. Once he sat down, however, his expression again became one of mask-like impassivity.

For an hour-and-a-half Ainsworth addressed the judges, who themselves listened to him with varying degrees of impassivity. He spoke fluently and rapidly and gave himself no opportunity of thinking beyond his actual words. If he should begin to do that, he knew that he would be lost, that his plea would be in danger of arriving at a stammering halt.

Apart from the judges, the lawyers and the court officials, there were only eight people in the court-room, and of these Ainsworth knew for certain that one must be from the Security Service. He had cast them covert glances and wondered which of them it was. But none had by so much as a small twitch indicated what his interest in the case might be. It gave him an uncomfortable feeling that one of them knew more about him than he cared to have known.

When at length he sat down, it was to hear the presiding judge say in a crisp voice, 'We don't need to call on you, Mr. Attorney.' The judge then went on to dismiss the appeal in as few sentences as could decently be used. He concluded, 'There was clear evidence on which the jury could convict and any other verdict must have been perverse. In these circumstances, this appeal is dismissed.'

While he was tying up his brief, an usher handed Ainsworth a note. He opened the piece of paper and read:

'I should like to see you. F.G.C.'

'Certainly, Mr. Ainsworth,' the presiding judge announced when he made the application to visit his client before he was taken back to prison.

As he picked his way down the narrow stairs, he wondered what Crofton wished to see him about. Though there could be

150

no more surprises to be sprung, he regarded the interview without enthusiasm, even with embarrassment. He was shown into a dingy room containing a small table and some chairs, and a minute later Crofton was brought in. The prison officer who accompanied him retired discreetly to the other end of the room and sat down facing them.

Crofton held out his hand. 'I hope you were not too cross with me, Mr. Ainsworth, for appealing without first consulting you. I am grateful to you for having agreed to appear for me in those circumstances. But I knew you would feel bound to advise me that I had no grounds for appeal'—Ainsworth was about to speak but Crofton held up a hand—'but the rules of my profession require that I should exhaust all the legal possibilities of release before finally submitting to my sentence.'

'Yes, I quite understand,' Ainsworth replied quietly. 'I'm sure you equally understand that it was rather a hopeless task.'

Crofton smiled sadly. 'I'm afraid it was. And now I shall shortly go off to one of your far from agreeable prisons, and you will be able to resume your holiday.' He looked reflective for a minute. 'I hope you don't mind my saying this, Mr. Ainsworth, but speaking for myself, I regret that we should have met under these particular conditions.'

'I endorse that.'

'I'm glad. That's kind of you.' He gazed round the uninviting walls and said with another sad little smile, 'In my profession there inevitably comes at some stage or another a sudden race against time. Whether one is then faced with years of imprisonment or given a decoration by one's government can often depend on little more chance than is involved in the toss of a coin. Did you realise that, Mr. Ainsworth?'

'I think I did.' *I realise it a lot better than you can possibly know,* he was tempted to add as the full force of the irony of the situation was borne upon him.

'It's an occupational hazard and I wouldn't want you to think that I'm complaining. My downfall is almost certainly someone else's triumph.' He suddenly looked very tired. 'But it'll now be for others to cut *their* pedestal from under them and send them toppling in their turn. It was a Frenchman, Mr. Ainsworth, who once likened aspects of our profession to the deep currents of the ocean. Powerful, tireless in their operation and always hidden from view.'

151

Abruptly he held out his hand. 'Goodbye, Mr. Ainsworth, and thank you for your help. I apologise if I've embarrassed you, but this is one of those moments when even a spy is inclined to become introspective.'

He turned smartly and walked over to the door. Then standing there with his back to Ainsworth he waited for his escort to come forward and open it.

For over a minute Ainsworth remained alone in the room, his mind obsessed by the irony of Crofton's unawareness of the events he had innocently wrought in the long-undisturbed life of his defending counsel.

As he slowly wound his way out of the deserted building, Martin Ainsworth reached the firm conclusion that spying was strictly for professionals. Though it seemed unlikely that his advice would be generally sought on such a matter, he would at least have no difficulty in following it himself.